D1808720

About the Author

Jonathan Reach is a retired professional who spent a lifetime in the law. His interests include golf, walking and playing music. He is a film buff with a particular interest in film noir and the nouvelle vague. He is a dedicated cricket follower, was a member of MCC for a number of years and played village cricket to an advanced age. As a writer, he has a particular interest in the psychopathology of behaviour and in the skills of litigation, in which he specialised throughout his legal career.

Rain Tests: The Return

Jonathan Reach

Rain Tests: The Return

Vanguard Press

Vanguard Press is an imprint of
Pegasus Elliot Mackenzie Publishers Ltd.
www.pegasuspublishers.com

First Published in 2025

Vanguard Press
Sheraton House Castle Park
Cambridge England

Printed & Bound in Great Britain

It is 2032, and the public is still thirsting for competitive cricket but global warming has ensured almost continuous rainfall.
New Zealand is back to compete with England and, hopefully, gain revenge for their defeat in 2028. This time, they will compete in five T20s and 3 Test matches. Bring on the rain!

CHAPTER ONE
RAIN TESTS – THE RETURN

After the hugely successful rain series between England and New Zealand in 2028, it was inevitable that the New Zealanders would want to come back for a return series.

They were still hurting from their narrow defeat, and considered their experience in the alien conditions would serve them well the next time.

The decision to resume play in 2032 was based on the precision now available in forecasting weather patterns up to a year ahead.

With a premium now placed on the relatively few dry days in each year – global warming having accelerated remarkably in the intervening three years – it was possible to schedule the fixtures with about a 99 per cent chance of rain.

Where they were still somewhat hostages to fortune was in the density and type of rain on any particular day, which could affect the pitch and occasionally result in abandonment, with the best will in the world.

Audiences for the previous tests, having started sparse, had increased dramatically towards the end of the series – even taking into account that all spectating was, of necessity, from undercover.

Having conferred over the previous two years, the two

boards had decided on a series comprising five T20s and 3 four-day Tests.

The extra day was a mere precaution in case of stoppages, as it was not expected that any of the Tests would last more than three days.

All matches would be played under lights, the power of which had been increased by about 100 per cent since the last series.

This would tend to accentuate the visual aspect of the rain itself providing an additional challenge to the batsman on each side.

In addition, after much discussion, it was agreed that the boundaries would be 60 yards for all matches, with a 25-yard fielding restriction for the first six overs in the T20s.

Test matches would commence at 11 a.m. and conclude at 4:30 p.m. or as soon as 60 overs had been completed.

A spare day would be allocated for each Test in case of necessary abandonment.

A number of the players on each side had been retained from the 2028 series, having gained valuable experience in the alien conditions. However, a number of newcomers were thirsting to try out their skills, particularly in the shorter form of the game.

For those readers coming fresh to this form of the game, there follows the rules, rainwear on the pitch, and some conventional terms used in the course of play.

CHAPTER TWO
THE RULES

1. Rain cricket shall only be played when rain is, in the opinion of the umpires, falling upon the wicket (the umpires' decision being final) and shall be suspended immediately upon rain ceasing to fall.

2. Rain cricketers shall, at all times on the field of play, be correctly attired; that is, they must wear an approved rain hat, rain jacket, and trousers, together with rainproof boots fitted with approved rain spikes of an approved type and length.

3. The area of the wicket shall be exposed to the elements at all times during a rain match and shall not be covered overnight or during intervals of play (save in exceptional conditions as agreed by the umpires).

4. It shall no longer be permissible to wear rain goggles fitted with wipers operating automatically.

5. All other rules of cricket shall apply to rain cricket, save that play shall not be suspended due to bad light or for any other adverse conditions unless, in the opinion of the umpires, such conditions could be considered as causing danger to the players.

6. Rain cricket shall be played with a white, rainproof ball. It shall be permissible for the bowler to clean the ball before and after each delivery.

7. The fielding side shall be permitted to wear rainproof gloves of an approved type.

CHAPTER THREE
RAINWEAR AND OTHER ITEMS

For those coming new to this novel form of cricket, we turn first to rainwear.

It had been agreed that cricketers should be:

a. Protected from the elements as far as possible

b. Neatly attired within the spirit of the game

c. Prevented, so far as possible, from becoming overheated or restricted by the rainwear, bearing in mind that freedom of movement is essential and that movement generates heat.

British rainwear specialists have created clothes with a unique blend of style, comfort and efficiency.

In heavy rain, the head is particularly vulnerable. Therefore, the first article of clothing conceived was a light, gently brimmed sloping hat that allowed water to run off the back and down the rear of a specially designed jacket.

A stretching-type hatband under the chin secured the hat.

Next, the rainwear jacket, again of lightest 'breathing' PVC, loose fitting under and around the arms, to be worn either with or without a conventional shirt – bowlers, in particular, demand freedom of movement in their shoulder and elbow joints.

The rainwear jackets fulfilled this function, being worn fairly long and overlapping with equally lightweight trousers of the same material.

The unique feature of the boots was their specially designed non-metal spikes, which provided instant grip on the ground and prevented slipping on soggy turf.

The spikes also assisted with the aeration of the pitch due to the factor of running up and down the playing surface, helping it drain quickly (umpires encouraged players to run up and down the pitch in rain cricket).

The rain cricket ball, is known as the 'plastic mac', being of apparently impervious white material with a conventional cricket seam, not susceptible to water yet soft enough to yield and not to damage the bat.

Cricket bats now came into their own. The poly-armoured bat of old adapted into a 'breathing' yet totally armoured surface. Its handle was bound with self-drying material causing no problem of grip for the new style impervious cricket glove.

Finally, umpires and wicketkeepers were carefully accoutred.

Umpires wore a one-piece rainproof outfit, hooded for the head and providing capacious pockets to provide space for the myriad items umpires hoard.

Wicketkeepers wore an outfit with built-in gloves and pads, lightweight but strongly resistant to impact with the ball.

There were, however, two previous innovations that were discarded:

First, the goggles worked by a battery to improve sight of the ball – a failed experiment that was soon abandoned.

Second and more significant, the 'attractor glove', which assisted fielders to cling onto the ball by assisting grip.

After a long argument, it was decided that fielders should be left as hostages to fortune in their efforts to catch a wet ball in the outfield. While it could feel like a lottery, at least the challenge would be the same for both sides.

CHAPTER FOUR
CONVENTIONAL TERMS

A. WET CRICKET SHOTS
- 'The Twizzle' a single run taken by running immediately when a ball is stopped at the foot of the batsman before the bowler and fielders have had the opportunity to see what has happened to the ball.
- 'The Fog' a hard shot hit into the air, confusing the fielder due to very poor visibility.

B. WET CRICKET DELIVERIES
- 'The Snorker', A yorker landing through wet and gloomy conditions on or immediately adjacent to the batsman's toe.
- 'The Splat', A ball aimed short through wet and gloomy conditions, designed to confuse the batsman by lifting water from the surface to disrupt their stroke.
- 'The Skid', On a wet but firm surface, a ball skids through fast and low, apt to gain an LBW decision.
- 'A Gloomer' usually a full toss, taking advantage of poor visibility and is a useful weapon for a slow bowler.
- 'A Waister' produced by skilful bowling on damp patches to get the ball up to waist-high or above, enticing a catch to close fielders.

CHAPTER FIVE
THE RAIN TESTS: SECOND SERIES

ENGLAND vs NEW ZEALAND
PLAYERS

ENGLAND

Ron Bridger (Captain)	Sussex	Right-hand batsman
Robert Grove (Vice Captain)	Yorks	Right-hand batsman
Jordan Clease (T20)	Lancs	Right-hand batsman
Geoff Pearse (T20)	Somerset	Right-hand batsman
Dudley Hardacre	Lancs	Right-hand batsman Wicket-keeper
Ray Pudsey	Glos	Left-hand batsman
Sam Devereaux	Northants	Right-hand batsman
Perry Hinchley	Surrey	Slow left-arm bowler, Right-hand batsman
Lawrence Power	Glos	Medium pace bowler, Right-hand batsman
Robert Lincoln	Essex	Fast left-arm bowler, Left-hand batsman

Jason Smethurst	Surrey	Fast right-arm bowler, Left-hand batsman
Roy Dukes (T20)	Yorks	Right-hand batsman, Left-arm leg-spinner
Patrick Hayes (T20)	Somerset	Left-hand batsman

NEW ZEALAND

Glenn Roach (Captain)	Wellington	Right-hand batsman
Forrest Smith (Vice Captain)	Central Districts	Fast right-arm bowler
Vance Whearby	Otago	Left-hand batsman, Medium right-arm seam bowler
Lew Pollard	South Island	Left-hand batsman
Jon Devenish	Wellington	Right-hand batsman
Robert Peters	Otago	Wicket-keeper, Right-hand batsman
Joe Potter (T20)	Wellington	Right-hand batsman
Ken Uttley (T20)	Wellington	Left-hand batsman
Tim Weatherspoon	Wellington	Fast left-arm bowler, Right-hand batsman
Rory Dunes	Central Districts	Fast right-arm bowler, Right-hand batsman
Leslie Oyami	Wellington	Right-hand batsman, Off spin bowler

| Peter Wright | Central Districts | Left-hand batsman, Leg-spin bowler |
| Joe Lymes | Otago | Right-hand batsman, Reserve wicketkeeper |

CHAPTER SIX
THE SERIES

GROUNDS

To prevent quagmires on the squares, a new type of resilient, fast-recovering grass was used throughout 2028 on the 'rain tracks', as they were known.

Most games occupied less playing time than their dry-pitch counterparts – those played in a torrential downpour turned out to be less than 10 per cent.

Brief spells of driving wet were used to the advantage of one side or the other. They unsettled the fielding side but disturbed a batsman's concentration.

The groundsmen tended to insert densely textured grass at the creases to give both batsmen and bowlers a firmer foundation.

Sight screens were dark for maximum contrast with both the white ball and the players' light-coloured outfits.

The press inevitably had a field day with the new expressions: *'the wet thrash'* for the final run chase and *'the damp squib'* for a game that simply petered out.

It should noted that One-Day Internationals had now become a thing of the past. The public had voted with their feet over the years for the thrill of the T20 or the longer delights of the hotly contested Test Match.

Bowlers on each side were allowed 5 overs maximum

with field restrictions for the first 5 overs.

NETS

In order to prepare the teams for the conditions as much as possible, indoor nets were provided at each playing venue.

Sprinklers and wind machines did their best to simulate the sort of weather that could be anticipated but, could not of course do other than give a semblance of what the payers would face out on the pitch.

THE MEDIA

Due to the paucity of normal cricket play in the wet conditions prevailing, media interest in the rain games was very high.

Sky had successfully bid for overall coverage of the T20 and Test series, while BBC2 was contracted to show a 60-minute truncated version in the evenings.

The games could also be followed online.

Trevor Ganes and Bill Norris were on hand before and after the games to interview the players and obtain their feedback.

CHAPTER SEVEN
FIRST T20

HEADINGLEY
25TH MAY

THE TEAMS

England	New Zealand	Umpires
R. Bridger (C)	G. Roach (C)	P. Short
	T.	
J. Clease	Weartherspoon	N. Talbot
	(VC)	
G. Pearse	J. Potter	
J. Turner	K. Uttley	
D. Hardacre	L. Oyami	
R. Dukes	R. Peters (Wkt)	
P. Hayes	P. Wright	
R. Lincoln	R. Dunes	
J. Smethurst	F. Smith	
P. Hinchley	V. Whearby	
L. Power	A. Pardoe	

New Zealand won the toss and chose to field.
Play commenced: 11:30 a.m.

CONDITIONS
For the past few days, there had been heavy, persistent rain

accompanied by a nagging east wind. This had tended to prevent the ground from becoming saturated, but there was the threat of squally, heavy downpours during the match itself.

Although this might cause severe problems for the side batting second, Roach felt inclined in the first match to see a score on the board that his side could chase.

They had brought some T20 specialist batsmen who, he felt sure, would be able to clear the modest boundaries.

There was a promising crowd huddled in the pavilion and wherever they were protected from the rain.

At eleven o'clock precisely, the captains emerged, giving the sky a quizzical once-over, followed rather gingerly by the two teams, eager to sample the conditions – of particular importance in rain cricket.

The floodlights were on full, highlighting the rain falling at the moment in a straight, downward trajectory.

Trevor Ganes and Bill Norris from Sky were on hand to chat with the captains about the prospects. Neither was inclined to be very forthcoming at this stage, but both anticipated a close contest.

CHAPTER EIGHT
THE MATCH

England	New Zealand
R. Bridger (C)	G. Roach (C)
J. Clease	K. Uttley
G. Pearse	J. Lymes
R. Grove	J. Potter
D. Hardacre	R. Peters
P. Hayes	L. Oyami
P. Hinchley	V. Whearby
L. Power	P. Wright
R. Dukes	R. Dunes
R. Lincoln	F. Smith
J. Smethurst	T. Weatherspoon

ENGLAND INNINGS

The New Zealand team stood out in their white trim.

A number of the team had figured in the previous series and knew what to expect from the conditions, although they were surprised and pleased to note that the intensity of the floodlights had greatly increased this time round.

T20 specialists Roy Dukes and Patrick Hayes looked on anxiously as Ron Bridger and Jordan Clease strode out to open the innings.

They were cheered to the rafters by the small crowd gathered in the pavilion.

Robert Lincoln – a last-minute pick as a fast left armer – marked out his long run.

The rain was falling steadily, with little wind, and visibility so far was adequate as Bridger faced the first ball of the innings.

It was acknowledged that an early 'snorker', bowled right into the blockhole, could be quite difficult to pick and get away.

Lincoln tried three of these in a row. The first two blocked, but the third, moving down the leg side, was expertly steered wide of square leg for the first boundary.

Bridger survived the rest of the over, including an obvious 'waister', dug in short, that showered him with water but was expertly parried.

At the other end, Weatherspoon – a veteran of the first series – prepared to come in off a shorter run but with equal venom from a very fast left arm.

While it was unusual for two of the same type to play together, the angle each created and the uncertainty of whether the ball would hoop in or move away kept batsmen honest.

Clease announced his intentions immediately, lifting a short ball over cover with a carved six. Attempting another, he managed to avoid the lurking fielder Oyami by a few inches for a single.

Lincoln came in for his second over at Bridger, who took on a rather shorter ball and drove it majestically straight to the pavilion. Shots along the ground tended to lose momentum rapidly, and he realised this by hoisting the ball over the bemused bowler by thirty yards.

Wright, leg-spinner, now came on, giving the ball plenty of air and producing two or three 'gloomers' – balls that could easily be lost in flight.

Clease was able to get hold of one before it bounced and almost hit a four to leg. It stopped just short of the boundary, gaining him 3 runs.

To the last ball of the over, however, he chanced a sharp single into the covers, where the lurking Oyami swooped and sent a fast throw to Robert Peters behind the stumps for a smart run-out.

(Clease: run out 10–18 for 1)

Geoff Pearse – a specialist T20 hitter – entered the fray, swinging his bat and looking suspiciously up at the swirling rain. Taking guard to Wright slightly out of his crease, he signalled his intentions clearly enough.

There were 3 balls left in the over. After parrying the first, he connected with a tremendous lofted drive over mid-off for 6.

To the last ball, he attempted another huge hit but sliced the ball in a gentle parabular to Oyami at cover – who nearly dropped the spinning wet ball but clutched it at a second attempt.

Pearse realised that he had tried to go far too early, unused to the conditions, and departed with his head down to the pavilion.

(Pearse: caught Oyami, b Wight 6–22 for 2)

It was time to steady the ship, and vice-captain Robert Grove was just the man for the job. Beginning slowly, he gradually asserted himself and missed nothing on the leg side.

The outfielders had been restricted for the first six overs as usual, and by then the score had reached only 36.

Try as they might, the NZ quickies could not penetrate Bridger and Grove's defences, interspersed with strong drives and cuts through the air.

The 50 came up in the eight over, and Bridger was just about to show his true flair for the conditions when he played all around a fast stcker from Weatherspoon and lost his off stump.

(Bridger – bowled Weatherspoon – 22–62 for 3)

Wicketkeeper Dudley Hardacre now entered, swinging his bat vigorously. His reputation for big hitting preceded him, and he was soon into his stride, hitting Oyami for a huge six over long-on, as Grove continued to keep the score ticking over with pushed ones and twos – sometimes with a twizzle – taking a cheeky single with the ball at his feet before the fielders had located it.

Hardacre perished as he had lived. After striking another huge shot off Wright over square leg, he was deceived by a ball that kept rather low from Dunes, which had him palpably LBW.

(Hardacre – lbw b Dunes – 12–81 for 4)

With the overs running out, Patrick Hayes, a T20 specialist batsman, came in down the order, hoping to insert some urgency into the scoring. Unhappily, he was undone by a fast yorker from Forrest Smith, who defeated his forward lunge to bow him for a duck. A large moan rose from the crowd, who had expected great things from him towards the end of the innings.

(Hayes – bowled Smith – 0–81 for 5).

Just as Perry Hinchley was settling in to revive the scoring rate, Grove survived on appeal a load shout for lbw but went on to hit two fours in a row.

Hinchley buckled down as the conditions suddenly worsened with some heavy rain squalls which made the ball difficult to pick up.

Weatherspoon returned and soon had Hinchley driving loosely into the covers for Oyami to take another catch.

(Hinchley – c Oyami b Weatherspoon – 15–99 for 6).

Cometh the hour, cometh the man.

Lawrence Power now strode in with no great history of success behind him but commenced to nudge and noodle singles in every direction, to the frustration of the fielders.

Grove was practically becalmed at the other end, finding it more rather than less difficult to get the ball away as he was served some high-class skidders and snorkers. When Powers was eventually trapped on the crease by Smith, the score had advanced to something near respectable.

(Power lbw Smith – 22–127 for 7).

Grove struggled on, but apart from a few lucky blows by Lincoln at number 10, the innings subsided to 138 in the 20th over.

A reasonable score – although the squally rain had returned in bursts, which would make batting difficult.

ENGLAND INNINGS

R. Bridger (C)	b Weatherspoon	22
J. Clease	run out	10
G. Pearce	C	
R. Grove	not out	36
D. Hardacre	lbw b Dunes	12
P. Hayes	b Smith	0
P. Hinchley	c Oyami b Weatherspoon	1
L. Power	lbw b Smith	22
R. Dukes	b Oyami	3
R. Lincoln	c Oyami b Wright	
J. Smethurst	lbw b Whearby	2

138 all out in 19.4 overs

B	2
Lbs	2
Extras	4

BOWLING ANALYSIS

Weatherspoon	5–0–35–2
Smith	4–1–39–2
Wright	5–1–36–2
Whearby	3–1–8–1
Dunes	2–0–12–1
Oyami	1–0–8–1

NEW ZEALAND INNINGS

The rain had become more intense as Glenn Roach and Ken Uttley took the field to open the New Zealand innings.

A cheer rose from some of their loyal supporters – a few from home but several living nearby.

Bridger had decided that the approach initially must be for all-out pace: 'snorkers' and' skiders interspersed with 'waisters' dug in as hard as possible to lift the spray towards the batsman.

Robert Lincoln, fast left-arm, paced out his run and came in to unleash a fast, full-length ball outside the off stump.

Glenn Roach had little time to square up to his shot but managed to steer a thin outside edge past the one slip, Jeff Pierce, and saw it just reach the boundary.

The rest of the over saw him get solidly behind the ball, sometimes at the last minute, as the driving rain made it hard to pick up the flight.

Jason Smethurst, fast right-arm came in off a shorter, rather diagonal run and aimed two full-length balls on the stumps at Ken Uttley.

He had been introduced as a T20 specialist, and before the end of the over had launched two huge blows for four over extra cover.

Robert Lincoln now returned and bowled two fast 'waisters' off a short length, rearing up at the batsman, who was able to prod them harmlessly at his feet.

However, after turning a full-length ball neatly off his legs for two runs, Glenn Roach was clean bowled, off stump, by a fastball that he clearly failed to pick up.

(Roach b Lincoln 6–15 for 1)

Now the expectation rose as Joe Lymes strode out, swinging his bat ominously. Another T20 specialist with a season's average back home of 65, great things were now expected of him. As luck would have it, the rain now eased to little more than a steady drizzle.

Sighting the ball became easier by the minute and the two batsmen began to lay about them.

By the end of the sixth over, when the two quickies retired, the score had reached 52.

Ken Uttley was perhaps the more prolific of the two, his favourite shot being a lofted straight drive for four or six.

It came as a surprise when Bridger, acting on a hunch, restored Jason Smethurst to the attack. He saw the batsman aim another swipe at a ball well outside off stump, and slice into the covers to be well caught by Roy Dukes.

(Uttley c Dukes b Smethurst 38–64 for 2)

Now Ron Bridger produced his masterstroke by recalling Robert Lincoln to the attack.

Joe Potter groped at his first ball moving away outside off stump but was hopelessly beaten by the second, which had impalpably lbw, not even meriting an appeal.

(Potter – lbw Lincoln 0–64 for 3)

Robert Peters did his best to steady the ship against some fine leg-spin from Roy Dukes, who gave the ball plenty of air as the rain returned infrequent squalls, making it hard for the batsman to concentrate.

Joe Lymes continued to attack when he could, but his rate of scoring had lessened considerably. Eventually, he attempted a rather tired slog and saw the ball loop to Roy Dukes in the covers.

(Lymes c Dukes b Lincoln 39–87 for 4)

There was comparatively little battling to come now,

and Robert Peters succumbed to another catch by Roy Dukes as he tried vainly to accelerate the scoring.

(Peters c Dukes b Hinchley 8–94 for 5)

Leslie Oyami, a veteran of the previous tour, tried to hoist Hinchley out of the ground but was bowled neck and crop third ball.

(Oyami b Hinchley 0–94 for 6)

Forrest Smith, with no great reputation as a batsman, was promoted up the order and did his best to keep the score moving, with Vance Whearby able only to block and nurdle the odd run to leg. But Vance Whearby was soon bowled, mistiming a shot to leg, by Lawrence Power, bowling a demanding slow-medium.

(Whearby b Power 3–99 for 7)

Peter Wright and Roy Dukes did their best to hold an end up as Forrest Smith flailed away – dropped twice off lofted shots in the slippery conditions, but both fell in quick succession.

(Peter Wright c Dukes by Hinchley 5–101 for 8)

(Roy Dukes – lbw Power 1–103 for 9)

It seemed that the team were doomed for defeat, but now Tim Weatherspoon, last man in with nothing to lose, swung lustily. Between them, he and Forrest Smith took the score to a respectable 131.

It was not to be. Weatherspoon swung once too often and had his middle stump removed by a fast 'snorker' from Smethurst, at which point the England boys heaved a sigh of relief.

It had been a good contest, and New Zealand were rueing the collapse following such a rousing stand from Ken Uttley and Joe Lymes.

NEW ZEALAND INNINGS

G. Roach	b Lincoln	6
K. Utterly	c. Dukes b Smethurst	38
J. Lymes	c Dukes b Lincoln	39
J. Potter	lbw b Lincoln	0
R. Peters	c Dukes b Smethurst	8
L. Oyami	b Hinchley	0
V. Whearby	b Smethurst	3
P. Wright	c Dukes b Hinchley	5
R. Dunes	lbw b Smethurst	1
F. Smith	not out	20
T. Weatherspoon	b Smethurst	10

136 all out in 19.5 overs

B	3
Lbs	2
Extras	5

England won by 3 runs.

BOWLING ANALYSIS

Lincoln	5-0-38-3
Smethurst	5-0-42-5
Hinchley	5-0-30-0
Power	3-0-18-0
Dukes	2-0-5-0

CHAPTER NINE
THE AFTERMATH

Few, if any, games have been so dependent on weather as cricket.

Over the generations, attempts have been made to protect the wicket, and sometimes not, leaving the batsmen to face a 'sticky' with the ball turning square – something few batsmen were able to master.

By 2032, weather conditions had deteriorated to the point where a normal outdoor cricket season was impossible, and the only alternative to rain cricket was an artificial game played under a huge dome. This had never really caught on due to the expense involved, so rain cricket had come to be accepted as better than nothing.

The England players were feted by their fans, who recognised the conditions under which they played, and the New Zealanders found that they were welcomed and entertained widely between matches.

It was planned to have a formal presentation, perhaps with royalty – during the test match to be played at Lords later in the season.

In the meantime, the teams prepared for their next T20 to be played at Durham, where conditions could be challenging, to say the least at the end of May.

CHAPTER TEN
SECOND T20

DURHAM
29TH MAY

THE TEAMS

England	New Zealand
R. Bridger (C)	G. Roach (C)
R. Grove (VC)	K. Uttley
J. Clease	J. Lymes
G. Pearce	J. Potter
D. Hardacre	R. Peters
P. Hayes	L. Oyami
P. Hinchley	V. Whearby
L. Power	P. Wright
R. Dukes	R. Dunes
R. Lincoln	F. Smith
J. Smethurst	T. Wetherspoon

New Zealand won the toss and chose to bat.

NEW ZEALAND INNINGS

The wind factor was something very much in the minds of the openers Glenn Roach and Ken Uttley as they strode out to the wicket.

The rain falling was modest, but whipped up by gusts

of wind, it would make it difficult to pick up the ball cleanly.

Jason Smethurst sensed the opportunity and came in, firing three fast and accurate snorkers, which Glenn Roach kept out with difficulty, followed by a skidder just short of the length.

Roy Lincoln was equally fast from the other end but tended to veer a little off-line down the leg side, giving Ken Uttley the chance to whip him away over square leg twice.

Glenn Roach gradually found his feet and sliced a four over Leslie Oyami in the covers, followed by a strong lofted drive which veered in the wind as it whistled past Robert Grove, who could only get a fingertip to it.

Ken Uttley seemed determined to make every ball count, but in taking a sharp single into the covers, was beaten by the golden arm of Leslie Oyami and narrowly run out.

(Uttley – run out 8–16 for 1)

Joe Lymes realised that concentration was key, and after twizzling a couple of singles, leaving the ball almost at his feet, he settled down to pick off ones and twos from the slow bowlers.

Jason Smethurst came in for his penultimate over and curled one back late into Glenn Roach's pads – he was plumb lbw and wasted no time on a review.

(Roach lbw Smethurst 12–26 for 2)

Joe Potter entered, staring at the sky with the dark clouds scudding across the ground. After heaving a four over mid-wicket, he fenced at a couple from Robert

Lincoln and was then clean bold aiming a rather agricultural heave over the leg side.

(Potter b Lincoln 5–35 for 3)

Robert Peters gave every impression of settling down to support Joe Lymes, who was now into his twenties and seemed to have realised just what shots were available in the conditions. The pair prospered briefly before Robert Peters was beaten by an outswinger from nowhere from Robert Peters and nicked hard into the slips

(Peters c Power b Lincoln 9–55 for 4)

Joe Lymes was becalmed by now, realising that he had to stay in to guarantee any sort of competitive score.

Leslie Oyami decided that he had a better attack, but after smearing a four past mid-wicket, he played all around a fast snorker from Jason Smethurst and heard the death rattle behind him.

(Oyami b Smethurst 4–59 for 5)

Vance Whearby twizzled a couple of singles before he was clearly unsighted by a slow, flighted gloomer from Perry Hinchley and was caught in two minds – and literally picked up at short leg.

(Whearby c Power b Hinchley 2–64 for 6)

Peter Wright and Roy Dunes did their best to hurry the score along, seeing Joe Lymes unable to get the ball off the square – his timing all awry. Peter Wright swung lustily to be bowled by Robert Lincoln.

(Wright b Lincoln 7–76 for 7)

Roy Dunes lasted for a while, plainly uncomfortable in the wind, and eventually chanced a run into the covers where he was beaten by a fast, accurate throw and easily run out.

(Dunes run out 12–90 for 8)

The end was nigh as Forrest Smith scraped up a few runs until he charged Robert Lincoln to be caught and bold.

(Smith c and b Lincoln 3–95 for 9)

Tim Weatherspoon – no batsman – played no stroke and was lbw to a slow snorker from Roy Dukes.

(Weatherspoon lbw Dukes 0 – Lymes not out 29)

NEW ZEALAND INNINGS

G. Roach	lbw Smethurst	12
K. Uttley	run out	8
J. Lymes	not out	29
J. Potter	b Lincoln	5
R. Peters	c Power b Lincoln	9
L. Oyami	b Smethurst	4
V. Whearby	c Powers b Hinchley	2
P. Wright	b Lincoln	7
R. Dunes	run out	12
F. Smith	c and b Lincoln	3
T. Weatherspoon	lbw Dukes	0

Total: 96 all out

B	2
Lbs	1
Extras	3

BOWLING ANALYSIS

Smethurst   5–0–30–2

Lincoln	5–0–35–4
Hinchley	5–0–16–1
Dukes	5–0–14–1

ENGLAND INNINGS

Although the New Zealand total was modest by normal standards, the exceptional conditions now facing England rapidly put it into perspective. The afternoon was, if anything, windier than ever, with a sullen sky sending down rapid showers. Nevertheless, the team had no choice but to face it out and score as many as they could.

Weatherspoon and Smith were relishing the chance to deliver their fast darts into the sodden ground. Ron Bridger faced up, and with the wind whipping across from off to leg, the first three balls from Forrest Smith pitched outside off and veered harmlessly outside leg for wides.

The batsman was aware that the bowler only had to pitch a ball sufficiently outside off stump for it to swing in and catch him lbw. Luckily, this did not happen, and in the second over, Jordan Clease was able to clip two full-length balls from Tim Weatherspoon to the leg boundary. He chanced a quick two to the next ball but fell into the trap of calling for a single to Leslie Oyami in the covers. The dart into the wicketkeeper beat him by a full metre.

(Clease run out 10–12 for 1)

Geoff Pearce looked uncomfortable from the start. He swung and missed twice, then luckily connected with a waister dug in halfway down the pitch, and it sailed over mid-wicket for six.

Forrest Smith had him in his sights and swung one

viciously in from the off, catching him bang in front.

(Pearce lbw Smith 6–19 for 2)

Dudley Hardacre was made of sterner stuff. He blocked two straight balls, then watched Ron Bridger, who had been becalmed for an over or two, his timing well awry. In attempting an off-drive, he sliced to the waiting Leslie Oyami, who gratefully accepted a simple catch at cover.

(Bridger c Oyami b Weatherspoom 12–27 for 4)

Perry Hinchley never looked permanent. Not having learned the lesson from Ron Bridger, he attempted an unwise slash outside off, and Leslie Oyami ran in and dived full tilt along the wet grass to catch him, inches above the round.

(Hinchley c Oyami b Wright 2–34 for 5)

Lawrence Power then decided to block as long as he could, while Hardacre carved away with not a little luck – but they say it favours the brave.

Tim Weatherspoon was not to be denied and cut through Lawrence Power's defences with a perfect snorker.

(Power b Weatherspoon 6–47 for 6)

Roy Dukes was spared the fast bowling, but Peter Wright was bowling slow high gloomers, which took some watching and tackling in the high wind. His reward was to see Roy Dukes totally deceived and bang in front.

(Dukes lbw Wright 4–57 for 7)

Robert Lincoln could hardly expect to achieve what his superiors had not, but he had a good eye and took advantage of a rare break in the driving rain to swipe away two good fours before Forrest Smith returned to remove his middle stump.

(Lincoln b Smith 8–65 for 8)

Patrick Hayes now came in nursing a bruised left hand but was quickly dismissed by Peter Wright for 1 run – the ball unfortunately cannoning back off his bat onto the stumps.

(Hayes b Wright 1–68 for 9)

Jason Smethurst promised little and managed with difficulty to scoop yet another catch to Leslie Oyami to end the innings.

(Smethurst c Oyami b Wright 0)

ENGLAND INNINGS

R. Bridger	c Oyami b Weatherspoon	12
J. Clease	run out	10
G. Pearce	lbw Smith	6
R. Grove	c Oyami b Smith	4
D. Hardacre	not out	15
P. Hinchley	c Oyami b Wright	2
L. Power	b Weatherspoon	6
R. Dukes	lbw Wright	4
R. Lincoln	b Smith	8
P. Hayes	b Wright	1
J. Smethurst	c Oyami b Weatherspoon	0

Total: 70 all out in 19.3 overs

B	2
Lbs	1
Extras	3

New Zealand won by 26 runs.

BOWLING ANALYSIS

Weatherspoon	5–0–20–3
Smith	5–0–18–3
Wright	4–0–15–2
Oyami	3–0–10–0
Dunes	2–0–4–0

THE AFTERMATH

Trevor Ganes and Bill Norris from Sky interviewed the two captains in the safety of the Pavilion. They accepted that the conditions had been really testing for both sides and that it had been valuable to put a score on the board before the worst weather came in. It had been a bowlers' day – with exceptional efforts from both attacks.

Joe Lymes was made Man of the Match for his plucky 29, which helped New Zealand to put up at least a competitive score.

CHAPTER ELEVEN
THIRD T20

CARDIFF
7TH JUNE

After an unexpected couple of days of fitful sunshine, a steady gloom descended on Cardiff as the teams prepared for another tough battle.

After the toss – which New Zealand won – there was a long consultation before the decision was taken to ask England to bat first. It was reckoned that the wicket, having partly dried out, might be susceptible to pace.

Ron Bridger and Jordan Clease strode out to find that the rain had briefly stopped, and there was a ten-minute delay before the clouds opened again.

Tim Weatherspoon marked out his long run and came into Ron Bridger with three or four full-length balls, which he played away easily enough for ones and twos.

At the other end, Forrest Smith tried to vary his length with a couple of waisters, which Jordan Clease played away through mid-wicket for four.

Visibility was reasonably good and the opening pair had put on 24 in the first four overs when Jordan Clease went back instead of forward to a length ball and was lbw to Forrest Smith.

(Clease lbw Smith 14–26 for 1)

Geoff Pearce emerged needing a good innings and commenced to play robustly, as the team knew he could.

The score advanced rapidly again, and 50 was passed in the eighth over.

Ron Bridger took a liking to Peter Wright and twice swung him for six over long-on.

All was going swimmingly until Geoff Pearce tried to slice Tim Weatherspoon over cover, where Leslie Oyami leapt high to his right, parried the wet ball, and eventually held the catch

(Pearce c Oyami b Wright 32–94 for 2)

Ron Bridger brought up his fifty with a strong push back past the bowler and had started to express himself freely when he too attempted a cut without quite getting to the pitch, and lofted Leslie Oyami an easy catch in the covers.

(Bridger c Oyami b Weatherspoon 58–105 for 3)

Robert Grove had been quite becalmed watching Ron Bridger, but in attempting his first run, slipped and was run out.

(Grove run out 0–106 for 4)

With two new batsmen at the wicket, the pace of soring slowed for a time.

Dudley Hardacre found his timing difficult against spin, with high bloomers a particular challenge from Leslie Ayami.

Patrick Hayes came and went straight away, chancing his arm to Leslie Oyami in the covers.

(Hayes run out 0–106 for 5)

It was no surprise when Dudley Hardacre misjudged an off-cutter and was lbw on the back foot to Smith.

(Hardacre lbw Smith 5–114 for 6)

Perry Hinchley was keenly aware of the overs running out, and swung a couple of lusty blows over square leg before slicing to Leslie Oyami in the covers and immediately berating himself.

(Hinchley c Oyami b Wright 12–123 for 7)

Lawrence power now came in as the heavens opened with a vengeance. He parried away for a single and a two a couple of skidders well up to him from Tim Weatherspoon, before inevitably seeing his off-his stump cartwheel out of the ground.

(Power b Weatherspoon 3–127 for 8)

By the time Roy Dukes reached the crease, the weather had abated somewhat, and he survived for a while before slicing to Oyami in the covers for another simple catch.

(Dukes c Oyami b Smith 6–135 for 9)

Seeing little hope of surviving, Robert Lincoln took the long handle to the slow bowlers and managed a six and a four. He was then bamboozled by a slow off-break from none other than Oyami – brought on as a surprise package – only to see it shave his leg stump. He survived!

Jason Smethurst got away with a couple of twizzlers, dropping the ball at his feet and running sharply, before he was caught and bowled by Forrest Smith, leaving Robert Lincoln not out on 13.

(Smethurst c and b Smith 5)

ENGLAND INNINGS

R. Bridger	c Oyami b Weatherspoon	58
J. Clease	lbw Smith	14
G. Pearce	c Oyami b Watherspoon	32
P. Hayes	run out	0
D. Hardacre	lbw Smith	12
R. Dukes	run out	0
P. Hinchley	c Oyami b Wright	12
L. Power	b Weatherspoon	3
R. Dukes	c Oyami b Smith	6
R. Lincoln	not out	13
J. Smethurst	c and b Smith	1

Total: all out 150

B	2
Lbs	
Extras	3

BOWLING ANALYSIS

Weatherspoon	5–0–39–4
Smith	5–0–46–3
Wright	5–0–42–1
Oyami	3–0–12–0
Dunes	2–0–8–0

NEW ZEALAND INNINGS

A respectable if not daunting total, which New Zealand felt could be achieved – but they would need a good start.

Glenn Roach and Ken Uttley reached the crease as a

heavy downpour abated, and they were faced with steady rain instead. Smethurst paced out his run in anticipation of some good carry, and so it proved.

Glenn Roach was faced with several fast storkers, two of which, down the leg side, he was able to steer to the boundary.

Ken Uttley, in need of a good score, was rather more circumspect and played each delivery carefully on its merits for the first few overs.

Robert Lincoln was dealing in short-pitched waisters for a time, which were parried quite comfortably by Ken Uttley, who managed to swing two of them away over the leg boundary.

The score progressed to 30 with no apparent alarms.

Robert Lincoln then bowled a full ball which Ken Uttley tried to drive but hit uppishly into the bowler's arms as he followed through.

(Uttley c and b Lincoln 12–35 for 1)

Joe Lymes was unfortunate to come in as the rain intensified, and after smearing a fore through cover past the outstretched arms of Joe Potter, was palpably lbw to a fast full ball from Jason Smithhurst.

(Lymes lbw Smethurst 4–41 for 2)

Glenn Roach continued to prosper through cover, while Joe Potter blocked the slow deliveries now offered by Roy Dukes. Eventually, he could not resist a swing and was neatly caught close to the ground by Lawrence Power at mid-wicket.

(Potter c Power b Dukes 7–49 for 3)

Robert Peters arrived at the crease in a quiet lull of the

47

weather, with visibility very much improved. He was immediately into his stride with cuts and glances and a twizzle or two, ably backed up by Glenn Roach, who was approaching his fifty. This was the best time of the innings, with a steady flow of runs, until Robert Peters chanced his arm to cover, slipped momentarily, and was narrowly run out.

(Peters run out 18–90 for 4)

Glenn Roach raised his arms to celebrate a rare fifty, but his concentration lapsed for a moment, and a fast snorker from Jason Smethurst crept under his bat onto the wicket. From the other end, Leslie Oyami joined in the general applause as Glenn Roach trudged towards the pavilion.

(Roach b Smethurst 51–95 for 5)

With two new batsmen at the crease, England saw the chance for a real breakthrough – New Zealand still over 50 runs short of their target, and the overs running out.

Vance Whearby saw the total pass 100 before he misread a slow gloomer – a high ball difficult to pick up in the rain – and was lbw to Roy Dukes, who leapt in the air in delight.

(Whearby lbw Dukes 6–103 for 6)

Peter Wright came in with determination to protect his wicket at all costs.

In the meantime, Leslie Oyami got away a couple of slogs to leg and one fine on-drive before he misread a full-length ball and was bowled leg stump by Robert Lincoln.

(Oyami b Lincoln 12–115 for 7)

Rory Dunes did not delay the scorers for long, again

failing to pick up the line of a gloomer from Roy Dukes and was lbw on the move.

(Dunes lbw Dukes 2–120 for 8)

Forrest Smith, as usual, swung lustily, and luck favoured the brave for a while until he too misread a very slow bloomer from Roy Dukes and was bowled neck and crop.

(Smith b Dukes 12–135 for 9)

The last rites for the innings were performed by Tim Weatherspoon, who was equally bamboozled by Roy Dukes and bowled for 3 to complete the innings.

It had been close – with New Zealand getting within 10 runs of the England score – but the difference was no doubt the contribution of Roy Dukes, who took 5 wickets.

NEW ZEALAND INNINGS

G. Roach	b Smethurst	51
K. Utterly	c and b Lincoln	12
J. Lymes	lbw Smethurst	4
J. Potter	c Power b Dukes	7
R. Peters	run out	18
L. Oyami	b Lincoln	12
V. Whearby	lbw Dukes	6
P. Wright	not out	10
R. Dunes	lbw Dukes	2
F. Smith	b Dukes	12
T. Weatherspoon	b Dukes	3

Total all out: 140 in 18 overs

B	2
Lbs	1
Extras	3

England won by 10 runs.

BOWLING ANALYSIS

Smethurst	5–0–39–2
Lincoln	5–0–41–2
Dukes	5–0–45–5
Hinchley	3–0–12–0

THE AFTERMATH

Trevor Gaines and Bill Norris from Sky spoke to the two Captains in the pavilion as they enjoyed a good strong hot cup of tea. It had been a closely fought contest, and Glenn Roach was fulsome in his praise for Roy Dukes, who he felt had used the conditions brilliantly.

The teams now moved on to Southampton in a week or so – with all still to play for in the five-match contest.

CHAPTER TWELEVE
FOURTH T20

TRENT BRIDGE
14TH JUNE

England won the toss and decided to bat first on what they expected to be the best wicket of the series. Surprisingly, the team had remained unscathed barring the odd cold throughout the games to date.

The wicket was known to be fast, and the openers expected a salvo from Tim Weatherspoon and Forrest Smith, and they were not disappointed.

Ron Bridger, in particular, was subjected to a series of fast deliveries which he bravely parried, getting away a few good hits during the first 3 overs.

Rory Dunes had taken over the duties of Leslie Oyami in the covers and proved an able substitute. It was not long before the temptation to cut was too much for him, and Ron Bridger sliced a hard catch to Rory Dunes as if they had rehearsed it beforehand.

(Bridger c Dunes b Weatherspoon 10–20 for 1)

Ron Bridger departed, shaking his head, to be replaced by Jeff Pierce in defensive mode. Jordan Cleese, meanwhile, was enjoying some luck against the quickies, which convinced Glenn Roach to switch to his occasional off-spinner Leslie Oyami.

Cometh the hour, cometh the man, they say – Jeff Pearce went back to one that turned surprisingly sharply into him, and he was bowled.

(Pearce b Oyami 7–32 for 2)

Robert Grove was made of sterner stuff and soon put Oyami to flight over long-on for six. He and Jordan Clease cut and carved for a while before Jordan Clease underestimated the turn again and sliced to Dunes, giving Oyami a second wicket, which he celebrated with a wild run up the pitch.

(Clease c Dunes b Oyami 30–58 for 3)

Dudley Hardacre joined Robert Grove, and Glenn Roach immediately restored Forrest Smith to the attack. Robert Grove had perhaps gotten used to spin and was slow on a snorker, falling leg before.

(Grove lbw Smith 31–75 for 4)

Leslie Oyami was now in the middle of a golden spell.

Dudley Hardacre tried to break the stranglehold only to slice to Roy Dunes in the covers.

(Hardacre c Dunes b Oyami 6–83 for 5)

Perry Hinchley joined Patrick Hayes and put bat to ball convincing for a while.

At the other end, Peter Hayes failed to read the spin and went back to Leslie Oyami, only to be caught smack in front of lbw.

(Hayes lbw Oyami 4–90 for 6)

It was difficult to see where the remaining runs would come from, but Peter Hinchley clung on with Lawrence Power as the overs ran out.

Lawrence Power went the same way as others and was caught one-handed at slip by Peter Wright off Leslie Oyami, now in his pomp.

(Power c Wright b Oyami 6–106 for 7)

Oyami had finished his spell of only four overs with a haul of five wickets.

The end was soon coming now.

Rory Dukes was quickly late on his stroke and bowled by Smith.

(Dukes b Smith 2–110 for 8)

Robert Lincoln went back instead of forward and was palpably lbw to Forrest Smith.

(Lincoln lbw Smith 1–113 for 9)

Jason Smethurst got off a two and a one before the returning Leslie Oyami turned one into his stumps to end the innings at a most disappointing 117.

(Smethurst b Oyami 3–117 all out)

ENGLAND INNINGS

R. Bridger	c Dunes b Weatherspoon	10
J. Clease	c Dunes b Oyami	30
G. Pearce	b Oyami	7
R. Grove	lbw Smith	31
D. Hardacre	c Dunes b Oyami	6
P. Hayes	lbw Oyami	4
P. Hinchley	not out	14
L. Power	c Wright b Oyami	6
R. Dukes	b Smith	2
R. Lincoln	lbs Smith	1
J. Smethurst	b Oyami	3

B	1
Lbs	2
Extras	3

BOWLING ANALYSIS

Weatherspoon	5–0–32–1
Smith	5–0–34–3
Oyami	5–0–40–6
Wright	4–0–6–0

NEW ZEALAND INNINGS

The England score did not, on the face of it, present much of a challenge, save for the pace of the pitch.

Glenn Roach and Ken Uttley strode out in the face of fairly persistent drizzle. The forecast was the steadily increasing rain during the afternoon. They concluded that a good start was essential.

Jason Smethurst was studying the sky with interest as he measured out his run. He was determined to give the New Zealand openers a roasting, it took them both a couple of overs from the quickies to settle down.

Robert Lincoln was intent on firing in short waisters but soon realised that they were quite easily steered away behind square.

Glenn Roach got into his stride with a couple of powerful straight drives over the bowler's head and began to gain confidence once the spinners took over.

The two of them had put on 30 together when Ken

Uttley got a thin outside edge to Lawrence Power and was caught at slip.

(Uttley c Hardacre b Power 14–32 for 1)

Joe Lymes announced his arrival with a rasping cut for four and was in no mood to hang about.

Ron Bridger brought Robert Lincoln back and was rewarded when Glenn Roach fenced at a sharp skidder and was bowled off-stump.

(Roach b Lincoln 25–42 for 2)

Joe Potter faced up and, after a huge swipe, was bowled off a thick inside edge for a duck.

(Potter b Lincoln 0–42 for 3)

Glenn Roach went to meet Robert Peters, and they conferred gravely before the batsman took guard. No doubt he had been advised that Robert Lincoln was on something of a role.

There was one ball left in the over, to which Robert Peters obligingly went back and was clean-bowled by a rapid yorker that came into him at the last moment.

(Peters b Lincoln 0–43 for 4)

Leslie Oyami breathed a sigh of relief to see Robert Lincoln taken off and replaced by the gentle spin of Perry Hinchley.

The rain had suddenly intensified, and a sharp wind got up, making it difficult to pick the slow, lofted gloomers from Hinchley.

After staring a loose ball on the leg for three, Leslie Oyami failed to cite a low full toss which bowled him off-stump.

(Oyami b Hinchley 3–49 for 5)

Joe Lymes had been very quiet through this carnage but now let loose with cuts and drives, ably assisted by Vance Wearby.

The score mounted rapidly, and Robert Bridger was unable to control it.

Eventually, Joe Lymes chanced a quick run to a ball into the covers, but was beaten by a swift throw and run out. There seemed to be no other way he was likely to get out in his present form.

(Lymes run out 35–90 for 6)

Whereas the England score had seemed to be mountains away half an hour ago, the situation had now changed dramatically. Peter Wright came in to face Lawrence Power but lasted only 3 balls before he was befuddled by a high, slow bloomer he failed to pick up.

(Wright b Power 2–96 for 7)

The game was now very much in the balance with about 3 overs to go.

Rory Dunes announced his arrival with a giant slog over square leg for 6, only to be run out risking a quick single to a ball which had barely left the square.

(Dunes run out 6–111 for 8)

Vance Whearby was now in control and, ably assisted by Forrest Smith, steered New Zealand home by two wickets.

(Whearby not out 25 – Smith not out 5)

NEW ZEALAND INNINGS

| G. Roach | b Lincoln | 25 |
| K. Utterly | c Hardacre b Power | 14 |

J. Lymes	run out	35
J. Potter	b Lincoln	0
R. Peters	b Lincoln	0
L. Oyami	b Hinchley	3
V. Whearby	not out	26
P. Wright	b Power	2
R. Dunes	run out	6
F. Smith	not out	5

Total: 118 from 8 wkts

B	1
Lbs	2
Extras	3

BOWLING ANALYSIS

Lincoln	5–0–39–3
Smith	5–0–25–0
Power	5–0–29–2
Hinchley	3–0–2

AFTERMATH

Trevor Gaines and Bill Norris were on hand for Sky as usual, and the captains once again praised the bowlers on both sides for their sterling efforts.

It had been a very close contest, and New Zealand had held their nerve at the end to pull off an excellent victory.

At 2-all, there was now everything to play for in the 5th and final T20 in Bristol, where there was sure to be a large and hardy crowd never afraid of a little West Country rain.

CHAPTER TWELVE
FIFTH T20

BRISTOL
25th JUNE

The weather forecast indicated steady rain throughout the day, giving little advantage to either side.

The captains went out to toss, giving a scowl or two at the heavy clouds above. Glenn Roach called correctly and did not hesitate in deciding to bat first.

New Zealand had picked the same 11 who had served them so well in the series so far. All seemed well after a bout of mild flu had affected half of them the previous week.

Glenn Roach and Ken Uttley emerged to great cheers from the crowd, who had come to admire the skills and fortitude of the visitors.

Jason Smethurst surmised that there would probably be low bounce on the Bristol pitch and the ball would need to be well-pitched up to do maximum damage.

Gell Roach was quickly into his stride with a clip for four off his legs and a powerful drive over the head of Robert Lincoln in the second over.

Ken Uttley seemed fairly skittish, and after some huge swings to leg, he took a chance too many into the covers and was easily run out, having been sent back by Glenn Roach at the last moment.

(Uttley run out 12–25 for 1)

Joe Lymes came to the wicket full of confidence after his last innings and began matching Glenn Roach blow for blow. He rapidly overtook Glenn Roach in the scoring, and the total had passed 50 when he drove and got a thin edge to slip.

(Lymes c Hardacre b Lincoln 27–59 for 2)

Joe Potter never settled, and having parried a couple outside of stump, he was bowled off an inside edge by Robert Lincoln.

(Potter b Lincoln 1–62 for 3)

Robert Peters prospered for a while and was beginning to time away the short balls when he advanced a little early to a slow gloomer from Perry Hinchley and was caught and bowled – the bowler juggling with the catch before securing it.

(Peters c and b Hinchley 16–76 for 4)

Leslie Oyami swung lustily and gave good support to Glenn Roach for a while. Ron Bridger then took a bold decision and brought back Robert Lincoln. Glenn Roach drove a little early and was caught low down at slip, cursing his luck as he departed for the pavilion.

(Roach c Hardacre b Lincoln 36–93 for 5)

Vance Whearby came in to face the returning Jason Smethurst and lasted only 3 balls before being comprehensively beaten and bowled.

(Whearby b Smethurst 0–97 for 6)

Laslie Oyami and Peter Wright flourished for a while, but Leslie Oyami was undone by another slow bloomer from Lawrence Power and bowled leg stump.

(Oyami b Wright 11–114 for 7)

The prospect of a large score was receding rapidly as Rory Dunes strode into bat.

Peter Wright was next to go, advancing up the pitch and giving Jason Smethurst a sharp catch low to his right.

(Wright c and b Smethurst 6–118 for 8)

Forrest Smith, as usual, resorted to the long handle and his blows came off for a while as Rory Dunes accumulated in ones and twos. Eventually, his luck ran out, and he snicked hard to slip, where a very good low catch was accepted.

(Smith c Hardacre b Lincoln 10–132 for 9)

Tim Weatherspoon was soon undone by another skilful gloomer from Lawrence Power to end the innings, with Rory Dunes 15 not out.

(Weatherspoon b Power 3)

NEW ZEALAND INNINGS

G. Roach	c Hardacre b Lincoln	36
K. Uttley	run out	12
J. Lymes	c Hardacre b Lincoln	27
J. Potter	b Lincoln	1
R. Peters	c and b Hinchley	16
L. Oyami	b Power	11
V. Whearby	b Smethurst	0
P. Wright	c and b Smethurst	6
R. Dunes	not out	15
F. Smith	c and b Lincoln	10
T. Weatherspoon	b Power	3

Total 140 all out in 18.5 overs

B	1
Lbs	2
Extras	3

BOWLING ANALYSIS

Lincoln	5–0–45–4
Smith	5–0–39–2
Hinchley	5–0–26–1
Power	3.5–0–27–1

ENGLAND INNINGS

There was tremendous excitement as Ron Bridger and Jordan Clease strode out to the wicket. There were thousands of umbrellas up in the crowd, among whom could be seen a number of small England flags waving. Never let it be said that a West Country crowd was not patriotic – and able to stand out cheerfully in all weathers. Their enthusiasm seemed to have translated itself to the two batsmen.

Ron Bridger was into his stride with a beautifully struck four through the covers, followed by an elegant turn to leg for a single. However, to the last ball of the first over, he played back, the ball took a deflection off his bat, and onto the leg stump. There was a roar of dismay as he trudged off to be replaced by Geoff Pearce.

(Bridger b Weatherspoon 5–5 for 1)

Geoff Pearce knew that the crowd was fully behind him and began to strike the ball majestically through extra cover. Jordan Clease followed his lead, and the two of them passed 50 within six overs.

Jordan Clease was taking a few liberties with Twizzles at his feet, and the running between the wickets seemed secure until he chanced a quick single to cover and was narrowly run out as he turned to try and regain his crease.

(Clease run out 45–72 for 2)

Robert Grove introduced a rather more sober note, getting well behind the various snorkers. He looked secure enough until he carved a high ball into the covers, where Leslie Oyami (who else?) leapt to his right and took a stunning catch at full stretch.

(Grove c Oyami b Weatherspoon 12–90 for 3)

Dudley Hardacre came in to face a change of bowling as Peter Wright bowled him some high gloomers, most of which he saw early and put away through mid-wicket.

Geoff Pearce was taking on Robert Smith and, having driven him imperiously over his head to the boundary, was late on a fast in-swinger and comprehensively bowled to end a fine innings.

(Pearce b Smith 38–106 for 4)

Patrick Hayes sensed that the game was now winnable, and he and Dudley Hardacre worked once and twos to the despair of Peter Wright.

Even the introduction of Leslie Oyami did little to halt the flow, and Glenn Roach was obliged to bring back Robert Smith for a final burst. This paid dividends as Dudley Hardacre missed a straight skidder and was plumb in front. He had played his part and was applauded for all the way to the pavilion.

(Hardacre lbw Smith 14–124 for 5)

Perry Hinchley was not going to let the side down

from here, and he and Patrick Hayes saw the side home without further alarms.

ENGLAND INNINGS

R. Bridger	b Weatherspoon	5
J. Clease	run out	45
G. Pearce	b Smith	38
R. Grove	c Oyami b Weatherspoon	12
D. Hardacre	lbw Smith	14
	Total: 141 for 5 wkts in 19.2 overs	

B	1
Lbs	3
Extras	3

BOWLING ANALYSIS

Weatherspoon	5–0–38–2
Smith	5–0–38–2
Oyami	5–0–36–0
Dunes	4.2–0–17–0

England won by 5 wickets

England won the T 20 series 3 games to 2.

AFTERMATH

Trevor Gaines and Bill Norris were, of course, enthused at England's performance with the bat, which they had been threatening all series. Ron Bridger was congratulated by Glenn Roach on England's victory after some very keenly contested matches.

There was an excited crowd in the pavilion, and the celebrations extended well into the evening, with Bridger breaking open the champagne and showering his players in the traditional manner.

Everyone now needed time to regroup and prepare for the Test series, which was bound to be enthralling and close.

CHAPTER THIRTEEN
THE RAIN TESTS – THE RETURN

PRELUDE

The first of 3 test matches between England and New Zealand was to be played at Lord's – the home of cricket. There was keen anticipation of this first of the 3 matches, as the players had by now seen a good deal of each other in the T20 series, which had been so closely fought and exciting.

On the eve of the Test Match, a reception was held at Lord's for the teams and their entourage, hosted by the President of MCC. This was a formal affair, and the players and their ladies were welcomed by a number of MCC committee members. After dinner speeches were made by the two team captains, and here are some extracts:

Glenn Roach (New Zealand Captain)
"It is a great privilege to be dining here at the home of cricket with the prospect of a Test Match in the next few days. I can only say that we as a team have been wonderfully treated as we have made our way around the country and have enjoyed great support from all sides as we have weathered the conditions.

Following our first speculative tour in 2028, when we

did not know quite what the reception would be, there is no doubt that rain cricket provides the rich entertainment that the elements would otherwise deny us, since the number of playing days available for normal outdoor cricket are increasingly fewer.

It remains for me to say on behalf of all our team that we are delighted to be back and hope this time to emerge victorious."

Ron Bridger (England Captain)
"I can only thank my opposite number, Glenn Roach, for his most generous and positive remarks.

As Captain of the home team for the second time in four years, I must first commend the excellent preparation of the pitches on which we have played around the country and in all weathers. We have enjoyed very good support everywhere, and I hope that we have repaid it by giving our spectators some rich entertainment.

I know that I and all the team are looking forward to the coming Test series with great anticipation.

May I conclude by thanking MCC and you, Mr President, for this excellent dinner and an occasion that none of us will ever forget."

THE FIRST TEST
LORDS

1ST JULY
DAY ONE

In the traditional way, the teams lined up on the sacred turf about thirty minutes before the start of play. The occasion was for the teams to meet and greet Prince William, who had lately shown a great deal of interest in rain cricket.

Large umbrellas were the order of the day for the royal guest, accompanied by the President and Vice President of MCC and several senior members of the committee.

The crowd had begun to thicken as the rain fell steadily, and a large black cloud began to drift in from the west. Ominous rolls of thunder were heard in the distance, and about the time for the start of play, the impending storm hit and large flashes of lightning lit up the sky. It was quite a thing of wonder and delayed the start for about half an hour until the umpires were convinced that the storm had truly passed with no risk of lightning strikes to the players

The captains emerged for the toss, and with England having won it Ron Bridger had no hesitation in deciding to field. He guessed that batting would be no joke on the soaked pitch, although the rain had now abated into a steady drizzle.

The England team took the field lit up by the dazzling lights which cast shadows across the pitch. Glenn Roach and wicketkeeper Joe Lymes strode to the wicket as Robert Lincoln measured out his long run. Glenn Roach played impeccably straight at the full-length snorkers held down and was able to drive through a slightly shorter delivery and see it raced to the cover boundary.

Jason Smethurst equally fancied his chances with balls well up but interspersed them with the odd waister dug in short and spraying the batsman as he stood up and played it away.

This was perhaps the best start New Zealand had enjoyed in the series and they passed 50 together with Joe Lymes enjoying a number of effective pulls for four to the mid-wicket boundary.

Ron Bridger had rested Robert Lincoln for an over but bought him back for a final burst which paid dividends.

Glenn Roach paid the price for going back instead of forward to a fullish skidder from Robert Lincoln, which caught him plumb in front – verified by an appeal which he lost.

(Roach lbw Lincoln 30–51 for 1)

Ken Uttley arrived as the rain started to intensify again, and a breeze had sprung up. He scarcely had time to play himself in when Joe Lymes was hopelessly beaten by a fast-swinging ball from Jason Smethurst and bowled off stump – which obligingly flew out of the ground.

(Lymes b Smethurst 22–53 for 2)

Joe Potter who had been retained from the T20s for

his striking ability – came in to face Lawrence Power bowling slow gloomers which he saw early and was able to dispatch two beyond the ropes at square leg.

In the meantime, Ken Uttley was taking chances with stolen singles and having tried this once too often was beaten by a throw from extra cover and run out.

(Uttley run out 10–60 for 3)

Robert Peters emerged to face Perry Hinchley at the pavilion end, bowling slow beamers and using the slope to bring the occasional ball back sharply from the off. Having sighted two of these he aimed a huge swipe at the third, mist and was bowled. This was a wasted wicket and Glenn Roach could be seen outside the pavilion with his head in his hands.

(Peters b Hinchley 0–60 for 4)

Leslie Oyami had clearly learned nothing from the previous dismissal as he advanced to a full toss and tamely drove it back waist high to a grateful Perry Hinchley for a duck.

(Oyami b Hinchley 0–60 for 4)

Peter Wright to the rescue as the innings were fading badly.

Joe Potter had been witnessing all this from the other end with something approaching disbelief. He immediately scaled down his ambitions for pure defence as the situation demanded.

Peter Wright was discipline incarnate as he played every ball strictly on its merits, stroking the odd loose one for ones and twos.

It was another hour before Joe Potter at last lost his

patience and snicked Lawrence Power hard to slip where Dudley Hardacre took a good low catch to his right.

(Potter c Hardacre b Power 19–98 for 6)

Vance Whearby came in with little reputation but strong determination.

While Peter Wright picked off the occasional bad ball he played as straight as he could – and as two fast bowlers were now limbering up, nobody gave him much hope of surviving for long.

It was another half hour before he succumbed – including a break for lunch – and Jason Smethurst flashed a few past him before he beat the bat and had him plumb in front.

(Wright lbw Smethurst 6–110 for 7)

It seemed that everything had gone right for Ron Bridger but there was the fight in the tail. Rory Dunes came in to present a straight bat and in partnership with Peter Wright, they slowly clawed the innings back into semi-respectability.

The weather was giving them no favours with frequent squalls which did little to help concentration.

It took the return of Perry Hinchley to unseat Rory Dunes who saw what he perceived to be a long hop, played too soon and was bowled.

(Dunes b Hinchley 21–135 for 8)

Forrest Smith realised that he had little to lose by swinging freely and got away with some lusty pulls to the leg before Ron Bridger bought back Robert Lincoln for a final flourish.

Swinging again, Forrest Smith managed a thick edge

into the slips, caught by Dudley Hardacre low to his left.

(Smith c Hardacre b Lincoln 14–157 for 9)

The formalities were completed by Jason Smethurst plucking Tim Wetherspoon's middle stump out of the ground, leaving Peter Wright undefeated on a valiant 35

(Weatherspoon b Smethurst 6–167)

NEW ZEALAND all-out 167

ENGLAND FIRST INNINGS

New Zealand could feel disappointed after a bright start to their innings.

Ron Bridger and Jason Clease took to the field in the middle of squally rain, but with the knowledge gained from observing the previous batting performance. The New Zealand bowlers had also learned what was likely to be effective on this wicket.

Tim Weatherspoon was soon into his stride, spearing snorkers and long half-volleys into the stumps.

Ron Bridger was equal to it and was especially severe on anything off-line. His characteristic drive through the covers was soon in evidence.

Forrest Smith, by contrast, was keen to impose himself, and waisters hitting the pitch hard caused Jason Clease some problems, although he managed to put two away firmly to the leg boundary.

The openers progressed with few alarms and reached 50 without much risk.

Glenn Roach was about to turn to his slow bowlers when Ron Bridger received a really wicked snorker which crept under his bat and bowled him middle stump.

(Bridger b Weatherspoon 28–52 for 1)

Geoff Pearce was greeted by the introduction of Leslie Oyami and his high-flighted gloomers, which he played with great care.

Jason Clease had been rattling along but now went back instead of forward to Forrest Smith and was lbw. It looked marginal to the naked eye but was upheld on review, where it appeared much straighter.

(Clease lbw Smith 32–63 for 2)

Robert Grove seemed to be unconcerned by spin and played Leslie Oyami and Peter Wright with great assurance.

The pair were adding nicely to the score when Geoff Pearce was deceived by a sharply turning off-break from Leslie Oyami, which spooned off an inside edge back to the bowler.

(Pearce c and b Oyami 23–91 for 3)

Dudley Hardacre was clearly intent on seeing the day out and watched Robert Grove, who had been playing the spinners with increasing confidence. This proved to be his undoing as he sliced an intended cut back onto his stumps.

(Grove b Oyami 33–118 for 4)

With two overs left in the day, Glenn Roach gambled on a last fling from his fast bowlers.

Dudley Hardacre had played himself in against the spinners but lunged at Robert Smith and carved a simple catch into the covers, where the lurking Leslie Oyami made no mistake.

(Hardacre c Oyami b Smith 12–130 for 5)

With this last wicket, any hope of a substantial lead

vanished.

England left the field with honours about even but a stern test ahead to gain a lead on the first innings on the morrow.

DAY TWO

The second day promised steady rain, with the wind whipping up late afternoon.

Peter Hayes and Perry Hinchley, both new to the crease felt the need to press on but had not bargained with the increased enthusiasm of Robert Smith, having ended day one on a high.

He lost no time on swinging a fast snorker into the toes of Peter Hayes, from where the ball careered into his leg stump.

(Hayes b Smith 0–130 for 6)

Perry Hinchley was perhaps unfortunate when attempting a quick single to Leslie Oyami in the covers, whose lightning throw to the wicketkeeper beat him by a good metre.

(Hinchley run out 1–132 for 7)

Lawrence Power had come in following the demise of Peter Hayes and had not yet got off the mark. He was now joined by Roy Dukes, and both had something to prove.

The deficit was still over thirty runs, but with the spinners now in tandem, there was some respite from unrelenting pace.

Both batsmen commenced to use the long handle and prospered for a time as the rain eased off. Both managed to evade the outstretched hands of various fielders as they quickly overtook the New Zealand score.

Tim Weatherspoon was brought back on and produced a very fast snorker which undid Roy Dukes.

(Dukes b Weatherspoon 22–168 for 8)

Robert Lincoln joined Lawrence Power, and as usual, smote the ball fiercely using his keen eye. It could not last, and he scythed a catch off the outside edge to Leslie Oyami.

(Lincoln c Oyami b Weatherspoon 12–181 for 9)

Jason Smethurst managed one mighty six off Peter Wright before being bowled neck and crop to finish the innings.

(Smethurst b Wright 6)

(Power not out)

England all-out 188

NEW ZEALAND SECOND INNINGS
England began their second innings with a deficit of 21 runs, which could prove invaluable in a low-scoring contest.

Glenn Roach and Joe Lymes took advantage of a temporary lull in the wind as the rain poured down steadily. Jason Smethurst was as fast and accurate as usual and gave Glenn Roach a number of anxious moments as he felt his way towards a respectable score.

For once, Robert Lincoln was somewhat below his best and speared a number of balls down the leg side, which Joe Lymes put away with ease to fine leg. The pair had progressed with increasing fluency to 48 when Joe Lymes aimed a carve outside off-stump and snicked a low catch to Perry Hinchley at slip.

(Lymes c Hinchley b Lincoln 31–48 for 1)

At least the team were now in credit, but satisfaction was short-lived when Glenn Roach played well inside a fast skidder from Jason Smethurst and was bowled off-stump.

(Roach b Smethurst 22–54 for 2)

Ken Uttley watched in dismay from the other end but shortly afterwards chanced a run to a shot apparently well wide of Lawrence Power, who threw himself to his right, scooped up the ball, and threw down the stumps before the despairing batsman could regain his ground.

(Uttley run out 5–59 for 3)

Joe Potter and Robert Peters found themselves starting their innings together and conferred mid-pitch to decide on their tactics.

The wind had begun to swirl around, and the rain had increased, but they both played straight and only took runs where there was little or no risk. The score slowly rose. Joe Potter had been finding the pace of Robert Lincoln difficult, and his timing was awry. It was not certain he had picked up the line of a fast snorker which caught him plumb in front on the back foot.

(Potter lbw Lincoln 14–74 for 4)

Leslie Oyami joined Robert Peters but had scarcely had time to adjust to the testing conditions when he played too early at a fairly short ball from Robert Lincoln and drove it fast and low to the bowler, who scooped it up as he fell forward.

(Oyami c and b Lincoln 2–77 for 5)

With the lead only about 50, it was time for batsmen to get their heads down, and to their credit, Robert Peters and Peter Wright cut out any loose shots and played commendably straight.

Together, attacking only loose balls and running fast between the wickets, they took the score beyond 100 to Glenn Roach's intense relief.

The slow bowlers were giving the ball plenty of air, and eventually, this paid dividends when Peter Wright lunged forward too early and lobbed a ball off the outside edge back to Roy Dukes.

(Wright c and b Dukes 30–125 for 6)

Vance Whearby decided from the start to present a dead bat and leave any scoring to Robert Peters. He was playing at his best now, and it came as a surprise when he misjudged a pull at a high gloomer from Lawrence Power and was beaten and bowled middle stump.

(Peters b Power 43–152 for 7)

Roy Dunes came in with the wind now gusting unpleasantly and the rain falling heavily.

Robert Lincoln lined him up after one heave for 4 and took out his leg stump.

(Dunes b Lincoln 5–160 for 8)

Forrest Smithy now attempted a suicide single and was easily run out.

(Smith run out 2–175 for 9)

Little was expected of Tim Weatherspoon in the conditions, and he popped a high gloomer back into the grateful hands of Lawrence Power to end the innings.

(Weatherspoon c and b Power 3)

(Whearby not out 10)
New Zealand all-out 172

ENGLAND SECOND INNINGS

There was time for only two overs as Ron Bridger and Jason Kleys strode out to face the two fast bowlers, with an over at each end to test their metal. Neither batsman was inclined to take any risks, but Ron Bridger seized on a loose ball from Forrest Smith had put it away through the covers.

The teams retired to consider their positions, with England requiring less than 150 to win the match.

DAY THREE

New Zealand took to the field, realising that something special would be required of them to pull off a win. A great deal would rest on the shoulders of the two fast bowlers.

Ron Bridger had shown the previous evening that he was going on the attack whenever he could. There were several more rasping drives which scorched past Leslie Oyami's hands at cover. Jason Clease, by contrast, was rather becalmed, scoring of ones and twos.

The 50 came up remarkably quickly, but Jason Clease, who had found Robert Smith a difficult proposition, now found himself in front of a rapid in-swinging snorker.

(Clease lbw 16–52 for 1)

Geoff Pearce was then late backing up Ron Bridger for a quick single. There was some confusion about whose call it was, but the outcome anyway was that Jeff Pierce was run out.

(Pearce run out 2–54 for 2)

Robert Grove was given a stern talking-to as he arrived to join his captain. However, it proved of little value, as the captain's valiant innings came to an end when he drove Tim Weatherspoon hard but at catchable height.

Dudley Hardacre knew that he and Robert Grove would need to do the bulk of the scoring from now on. They progressed cautiously for a while until Robert Grove sliced a cut straight to Leslie Oyami, who gratefully received it in the covers.

(Grove c Oyami b Weatherspoon 15–77 for 4)

Peter Hayes arrived to play what turned out to be the defining innings for England.

Dudley Hardacre progressed for a while and played some good drives before he, too, sliced to Leslie Iyami in the covers.

(Hardacre c Oyami b Smith 20–95 for 5)

Perry Hinchley was determined to give good support and was gratified to note that Peter Hayes seemed to have the better of the slow bowlers, milking them for once and twos as his score progressed towards 30.

Perry Hinchley, however, was guilty of being slow to respond to a call for a single and was run out by a whisker.

(Hinchley run out 12–125 for 6)

Lawrence Power never looked confident facing Tim Weatherspoon.

New Zealand had realised that they still had a chance to pull off a great victory if they could topple England for less than 150, and the outcome lay in the hands of the fast bowlers.

After steering a 4 behind square, Lawrence Power was beaten and bowled by Tim Wetherspoon to the great delight of the surrounding fielders.

(Power b Weatherspoon 4–132 for 7)

Roy Dukes came in to find fielders all around the bat as Peter Wright wheeled in and tested him with some tantalising slow gloomers. To the last all of an over, he played back to a shorter ball, which thudded into his pads.

The loud appeal for lbw was upheld.

(Dukes lbw Wright 3–141 for 8)

With only 10 required, Peter Hayes swiftly put bat to ball and drove two fours to the mid-wicket boundary. Robert Lincoln scrambled a single and left Peter Hayes to win the match with a glide to leg for two.

England 151 for 8 wickets.

England won by 2 wickets.

NEW ZEALAND FIRST INNINGS

G. Roach	lbw Lincoln	30
J. Lymes	b Smethurst	22
K. Uttley	run out	10
J. Potter	c Hardacre b Power	19
R. Peters	b Hinchley	0
L. Oyami	c and b Hinchley	0
P. Wright	not out	35
V. Whearby	lbw Smethurst	6
R. Dunes	b Hinchley	21
F. Smith	c and b Lincoln	5
T. Weatherspoon	b Smethurst	6

Total 167 all-out

B	2
Lbs	2
Extras	4

BOWLING ANALYSIS

Lincoln	5–0–47–2

Smethurst	5–0–39–3
Hinchley	5–0–42–3
Power	5–0–35–1

ENGLAND FIRST INNINGS

R. Bridger	b Weatherspoon	28
J. Clease	lbw Smith	32
G. Pearce	c and b Oyami	33
R. Grove	b Oyami	33
D. Hardacre	c Oyami b Smith	12
P. Hayes	b Smith	0
P. Hinchley	run out	1
L. Power	not out	14
R. Dukes	b Weatherspoon	22
R. Lincoln	c Oyami b Weatherspoon	12
J. Smethurst	b Wright	6

Total 188 all out

B	3
Lbs	2
Extras	5

BOWLING ANALYSIS

Weatherspoon	5–0–49–3
Smith	5–0–46–3
Oyami	5–0–42–2
Wright	5–0–46–1

NEW ZEALAND SECOND INNINGS

G. Roach	b Smethurst	22
J. Lymes	c Hinchley b Lincoln	31

K. Uttley	run out	5
J. Potter	lbw Lincoln	14
R. Peters	b Power	43
L. Oyami	c and b Lincoln	2
P. Wright	c and b Dukes	30
V. Whearby	not out	10
R. Dunes	b Lincoln	5
F. Smith	run out	2
T. Weatherspoon	c and b Power	3

Total 172 all out

B	3
Lbs	2
Extras	5

BOWLING ANALYSIS

Lincoln	5–0–43–4
Smethurst	5–0–41–1
Power	5–0–48–2
Dukes	5–0–45–1

ENGLAND SECOND INNINGS

R. Bridger	c and b Weatherspoon	40
J. Clease	lbw Smith	16
G. Pearce	run out	2
R. Grove	c Oyami b Weatherspoon	15
D. Hardacre	c Oyami b Weatherspoon	20
P. Hayes	not out	35
P. Hinchley	run out	12
L. Power	b Weatherspoon	4
R. Dukes	lbw Wright	3

R. Lincoln   not out   1

Total 151 for 8 wkts in 19.2 overs

B	2
Lbs	1
Extras	3

BOWLING ANALYSIS

Weatherspoon	5–0–38–3
Smith	5–0–3–41–2
Wright	5–0–40–1
Oyami	4.2–0–29–0

England won the first test by 2 wickets.

AFTERMATH

Trevor Gaines and Bill Norris from Sky were on hand, as usual, to congratulate the winning captain and commiserate with the loser – particularly as the game had been so closely fought.

Lords was packed with well-wishes for both sides, and the crowd was slow to disperse.

Ron Bridger congratulated all his players but reserved a special word for the gritty performance of Peter Hayes, who had held the second innings together and ensured victory in the end.

The teams now moved on to Edgbaston for the eagerly awaited second test.

THE SECOND TEST

BIRMINGHAM
15TH JULY

Rather unusually, there had been three dry days in succession before the test was due to start.

However, a heavy thunderstorm on the evening before was followed by a steady rain falling as the 15th July dawned. Both sides felt that this was going to be a good batting pitch with plenty of carry. An excited crowd had gathered in the pavilion, and the usual stallholders were at work around the ground. Although the air was muggy, they were doing a fair trade in hot food.

Glenn Roach and Ron Bridger gathered with the officials on the outfield for the toss, which New Zealand won. Glenn Roach had little difficulty in deciding to bat first, hoping to put a decent score on the board while the weather was fairly bland.

To a smattering of applause, the England fielders came out onto the pitch and viewed the sky. Glenn Roach and Joe Lyons followed as Jason Smethurst measured out a long run from the pavilion end.

For the first few overs, the ball came sweetly onto the bat with the bowling usually well up.

Glenn Roach was able to steer a couple of fours

through mid-wicket and one scorching off-drive, which beat the fielder standing fairly deep.

Joe Lymes waited for the bad ball to be put away, glancing a couple of times behind square. By the time the pair had put on 50, the slow bowlers were wheeling away, the high gloomers causing little problem.

Ron Bridger decided to bring back his fast bowlers for a second spell, and this at last paid dividends.

Joe Lymes drove hard at a ball well up to him from Jason Smethurst and edged it to Dudley Hardacre at slip.

(Lymes c Hardacre b Lincoln 23–55 for 1)

Ket Uttley played Robert Lincoln carefully but was disappointed to see Glenn Roach going back instead of forward to a fast snorker from Jason Smethurst, which took out his off-stamp.

(Roach b Smethurst 41–66 for 2)

Robert Peters was met with several high gloomers from Lawrence Power, which he swatted away, but then misjudged a shorter and quicker delivery which found him well in front.

An appeal showed he was banged to rights, and he drudged off, to be replaced by Joe Potter.

(Peters lbw Power 10–78 for 3)

Joe Potter commenced milking the slow bowling for ones and twos without risk, but Ken Uttley had lost his timing and attempted a drive at Perry Hinchley, which he could only snick to Dudley Hardacre, who took a good catch low to his right at slip.

(Uttley c Hardacre by Hinchley 14–97 for 4)

Leslie Oyami never seemed to settle at all and, after

one lucky slice through the covers, was undone by a slow gloomer from Lawrence power and clean bowled.

(Oyami b Power 4–104 for 5)

At least his side had passed the 100 mark, and Glenn Roach was quietly hopeful of a recovery as Peter Wright joined Joe Potter.

Peter Wright was into his stride immediately, with two sumptuous off-drives to the boundary and one straight hit into the pavilion.

The slow bowlers were suffering at this stage, and Peter Wright had only himself to blame when he was sent back for a dodgy single by Joe Potter and run out.

(Wright run out 19–117 for 6)

Vance Whearby decided that all he could do, as the rain intensified, was to block and support Joe Potter as long as he could. A worthy objective, but Robert Lincoln had other ideas, curling one in and bowling him behind his legs as he moved too far across his stumps.

(Whearby b Lincoln 4–123 for 7)

Rory Dunes came in during the worst of the weather as a sharp wind had got up, which made concentration difficult. He buckled down to it, but by now Joe Potter was taking some risks and shortly drove hard and snicked Jason Smethurst to Dudley Hardacre for a straightforward catch at slip.

(Potter c Hardacre b Smethurst 29–146 for 8)

Forrest Smith sliced a quick two into the covers before he, too, drove hard and edged to Dudley Hardacre.

(Smith c Hardacre b Smethurst 62–153 for 9)

Tim Weatherspoon did his best to lend support to Rory

Dunes, and they edged the score up until Tim Weatherspoon could not resist a huge swing and had his middle stump removed by a fast, shorter ball from Lawrence Power to end the innings.

(Weatherspoon b Power 4)

(Dunes not out 12)

New Zealand all-out 165

ENGLAND FIRST INNINGS

England could feel reasonably satisfied with their efforts in the field – they had never let New Zealand run away with the scoring.

Ron Bridger and Jason Clease strode to the wicket with confidence. The rain was steady, and the wind fairly mild.

Forrest Smith prepared to come in from the pavilion end, and Ron Bridger took guard to face him. The first 3 balls were well-directed and played back with a very straight bat. However, the fourth ball swung in late and caught Ron Bridger in front with little argument. Surprisingly, this was his first failure in the series so far.

(Bridger lbs Smith 0–0 for 1)

It was fairly late by now in the afternoon, and the floodlights were on full power as Geoff Pierce came in to join Jason Clease, who had yet to get off the mark. It was a slow process as they adjusted to the pace of the quickies, and the score rose to 20. There were occasional scares but nothing major. The shock of Ron Bridge's departure took time to wear off.

The slow bowlers came on and tried a number of

gloomers, but by now, both batsmen were into their stride and put away a number of boundaries.

The 50 came up with the batsmen now playing a number of shots, although Leslie Oyami was hovering as ever at cover and nearly got his hands to a carved shot for four by Geoff Pierce. Eventually, he tried another cut, but this time found Leslie Oyami equal to it, and departed, having played really well.

(Pearce c Oyami b Weatherspoon 32–55 for 2)

Robert Grove had taken his cue from Jason Clease and attempted a short single into the off-side. It was a serious mistake, as Leslie Oyami swooped in and threw down the wicket in one movement.

(Grove run out 1–58 for 3)

Dudley Hardacre could see the clouds gathering and the rain starting to increase. He was intent to support Jason Clease, who was driving the ball with complete confidence and hooking cleanly.

They prospered together for a while, but Jason Clese began to take risks and played over a fast sorcerer from Tim Weatherspoon.

(Clease b Weatherspoon 48–98 for 4)

Peter Hayes struck a two through mid-wicket to bring up the 100.

Dudley Hardacre had taken a liking to the slingers of Rory Dunes and put him away for two fours to fine leg, beating the fielder each time.

Peter Hayes then attempted a cut through the covers, got a thick edge, and was easily caught by Leslie Oyami running. There were only two overs left in the day when

Perry Hinchley came to the wicket – Ron Bridger had decided against having a night watchman.

Forrest Smith was brought back for a final dash, and his third ball moved late off the pitch and found Dudley Hardacre late on his stroke – the middle stump obligingly flew out of the ground.

(Hardacre b Smith 29–129 for 6)

With two new batsmen to start the second day together, the game was very much in the balance, with England still some thirty runs behind.

SECOND DAY

The overnight wind had somewhat abated, but the rain persisted steadily as Perry Hinchley and Lawrence Power took their places at the wicket.

Weatherspoon ran in fast, testing Perry Hinchley with a couple of fast skidders well up to him. He survived and Lawrence Power, after a few scares, also managed to settle in. Lawrence Power put away a couple of balls down the legside from Tim Weatherspoon before he cut uppishly and found Leslie Oyami pouch the catch at full stretch in the covers.

(Power c Oyami b Weatherspoon 15–155 for 7)

England had now almost reached parity – they could they go on and gain a useful lead?

Roy Dukes came in with all guns blazing, hammering two fours through mid-off and risked a quick single, which proved his undoing as the bowler swooped and bet him to the crease with a sharp throw.

(Dukes run out 12–170 for 8)

It was now all up to Peter Hinchley, who had hung on gamely seeing wickets tumble around him.

Robert Lincoln was no match for the wiles of Leslie Oyami, soon played all around a sharply spinning ball.

(Lincoln b Oyami 1–176 for 9)

Jason Smethurst managed to smear 3 runs through the

leg side, but Forest Asmith knew he only had to bowl straight.Sure enough, he struck Smethurst's pads to bring the innings concluded.

Still, England had secured a small but precious lead.

(Smethurst lbw Smith 3)

(Hiunchley not out 25)

England all out 184.

NEW ZEALAND SECOND INNINGS

There was time before lunch, for two overs and Jason Smethurst was fired up to bowl flat out at Glenn Roach. He survived the onslaught, and he and Joe Lymes went into lunch relieved to be able to start again.

Glenn Roach resumed in fine fettle, driving hard through the covers and never failing to hook short and fast deliveries for four.

Joe Lymes followed suit and was just beginning to blossom when he was sent back too late from a sharply taken single and run out.

(Lymes run out 10–35 for 1)

Ken Uttley played fluently from the start and surprised the fielders by driving a short ball from Lawrence Power into the pavilion for six.

The 50 was quickly passed, and Glenn Roach had just driven majestically through the covers for four when he drove again, got a thick edge, and was pouched by Hardacre at slip.

(Roach c Hardacre b Lincoln 45–69 for 2)

Robert Peters came in as the slow bowlers were finding their rhythm and at first, he found it difficult to pick up the line of a number of gloomers.

It was no surprise when he misjudged a low, looping delivery and was caught on the crease.

(Peters lbw Power 14–90 for 3)

There were 3 overs left for Joe Potter to face. However, it was Ken Uttley who cursed himself for not surviving the day when he drove hard and got an outside edge to the ever-lurking Dudley Hardacre.

(Uttley c Hardacre b Smethurst 39–118 for 4)

Joe Potter retired not out, ready to resume in the morning with the lower order.

THIRD DAY

The morning began with a violent thunderstorm which lasted a mere fifteen minutes. There was a ten-minute delay while the umpires inspected the pitch which had drained remarkably well.

Joe Potter and Leslie Oyami strode out, hoping to add some substance to the innings. They progressed in fits and starts, but the score crept up and it was something of a surprise when Joe Potter played right outside a fast soccer from Robert Lincoln and was bowled off stump.

(Potter b Lincoln 38–152 for 5)

Peter Wright joined Leslie Oyami, realising that their lead was now only 130 with little battling to come. They proceeded warily taking some sharp singles when offered, but Peter Wright tried a sharp 1 and failed to beat a throw from Robert Grove.

(Wright run out 14–167 for 6)

Vance Whearby always felt that he could bat-belying his lowly place in the order. He now proved his point with a very disciplined innings.

Leslie Oyami had meanwhile lived a charmed life having been dropped twice and now found himself facing a fired-up Jason Smethurst who darted a fast one into his pads.

(Oymai lbw Smethurst 12–172 for 7)

Rory Dunes was in no mood to hang about and swept a couple of fours off his legs. He then smote Robert Lincoln for a cheeky four back over his head but it could not last and he went back to a fast skidder and was bowled neck and crop.

(Dunes b Lincoln 15–198 for 8)

Vance Whearby was holding the fort and sneaking the odd single, knowing that not much was likely to be forthcoming from Forrest Smith or Tim Wetherspoon. He was quite right as Forrest Smith after a lucky swipe for 3 runs snicked hard to Dudley Hardacre and was caught behind.

(Smith c Hardacre b Power 3–210 for 9)

Tim Wetherspoon did his best to play a straight bat for an over to support Vance Whearby but perished swiping at Robert Smith to end the innings.

Still, a lead of close to 200 would give them plenty to bowl at.

(Weatherspoon b Smith 1)

(Whearby not out 22)

New Zealand 217 all out.

ENGLAND SECOND INNINGS

Shortly before lunch, Ron Bridger and Jason Clease strode out to bat a second time, their aim being 199 to win the match. They made a reasonable start and both had hit fours off the fast bowlers when they retired for lunch.

After the interval, Ron Bridger decided to play his strokes and powered a couple of fours through extra cover and a well picked-up six over square leg. Jason Clease had found it hard to get into his stride and was not timing the ball at all well. He seized on a waister from Robert Smith a tried to cut it hard only to spoon a catch to Leslie Oyami lurking as usual in the covers.

(Clease c Oyami b Smith 12–30 for 1)

Geoff Pearce was in good form and started to play well off his legs and drive straight whenever he could. He and Ron Bridger passed fifty and were going really well when Geoff Pearce was far too slow having been sent back for a risky single.

(Pearce run out 33–66 for 2)

Robert Grovetoo up the cudgels and realised that with the rain and wind increasing there was no point in hanging around. He too played some lovely shots through mid-off and his captain was going equally well.

Then disaster struck. Ron Bridger slipped in going forwards to a fast skidder and was bowled by Tim Weatherspoon who ran up the pitch whooping with delight as New Zealand now sensed that this could be a turning point.

(Bridger b Weatherspoon 36–87 for 3)

Dudley Hardacre was not really sure whether to attack or defend. He played tentatively for a time, surviving one sharp call for lbw. He was in two minds and drove uppishly at Tim Weatherspoon who caught the ball below the knee and celebrated again rather noisily.

(Hardacre c and b Weatherspoon 10–98 for 4)

Peter Hayes helped Robert Grove to put up the 100, which was a relief. Robert Grove was playing forward to all the straight fastballs but now went back to Forrest

Smith and was bowled off an inside edge.

(Grove b Smith 29–128 for 5)

A great deal now turned on how the lower order would respond with a maximum of fifteen overs left in the match.

Perry Hinchley did his best to keep the score moving with some good sweeps but ran himself out just as he was blossoming

(Hinchley run out 15–140 for 6)

Lawrence Power had no option but to strike out and was lucky to evade the fielders with two sliced shots for four.

Peter Hayes, who had shown great restraint up to this point, then tried to cut a short ball and inevitably sliced to the waiting Leslie Oyami.

(Hayes c Oyami b Wright 14 158 for 7)

The overs were now running out. Roy Dukes came and went swinging at a straight snorker from Forrest Smith.

(Dukes b Smith 2–170 for 8)

Robert Lincoln perished as usual after smearing a single being caught plumb in front.

(Lincoln lbw Weatherspoon 1–173 for 9)

With a final over to survive, Jason Smethurst thrust out a pad to the first 3 balls which were mercifully wide, barely missed the fourth outside off stump, and planted his bat firmly to the final couple of balls.

(Power not out 20 Smethurst not out 3)

England 180 for 9 wickets

NEW ZEALAND FIRST INNINGS

G. Roach	b Smethurst	41
J. Lymes	c Hardacre b Lincoln	23
K. Uttley	c Hardacre b Hinchley	14
R. Peters	lbw Power	10
J. Potter	c Hardacre b Smith	29
L. Oyami	b Power	4
P. Wright	run out	19
V. Whearby	b Lincoln	4
R. Dunes	not out	12
F. Smith	c Hardacre b Smethurst	2
T. Weatherspoon	b Power	4

Total 165 all out

B	1
Lbs	2
Extras	3

BOWLING ANALYSIS

Smethurst	10–3–34–3
Lincoln	9–4–46–2
Hinchley	136–42–1
Power	7–2–35–1

ENGLAND FIRST INNINGS

R. Bridger	lbw Smith	0
J. Clease	b Weatherspoon	48
G. Pearce	c Oyami b Weatherspoon	32
R. Grove	run out	1
D. Hardacre	b Smith	29
P. Hayes	c Oyami b Dunes	14

P. Hinchley	not out	25
L. Power	c Oyami b Weatherspoon	15
R. Dukes	run out	12
R. Lincoln	b Oyami	1
J. Smethurst	lbw Smith	3

Total: 184 all-out

B	1
Lbs	3
Extras	4

BOWLING ANALYSIS

Smith	10–4–41–3
Weatherspoon	12–3–52–3
Oyami	7–2–48–1
Dunes	5–1–39–1

NEW ZEALAND SECOND INNINGS

G. Roach	c Hardacre b Lincoln	45
J. Lymes	run out	41
K. Uttley	c Hardacre b Smethurst	39
J. Potter	b Lincoln	38
R. Peters	lbw Power	14
L. Oyami	lbw Smethurst	12
P. Wright	run out	14
V. Whearby	not out	22
R. Dunes	b Lincoln	15
F. Smith	c Hardacre b Power	3
T. Weatherspoon	b Smethurst	3

Total: 217 all-out

B	1
Lbs	3
Extras	4

BOWLING ANALYSIS

Smethurst	13–3–56–3
Lincoln	13–4–58–3
Power	15–3–54–2
Hinchley	10–2–45–0

ENGLAND SECOND INNINGS

R. Bridger	b Weatherspoon	36
J. Clease	c Oyami b Smith	12
G. Pearce	run out	33
R. Grove	b Smith	29
D. Hardacre	c and b Weatherspoon	10
P. Hayes	c Oyami b Wright	14
P. Hinchley	run out	15
L. Power	not out	20
R. Dukes	b Smith	2
R. Lincoln	lbw Weatherspoon	1
J. Smethurst	not out	3

Total: 180 for 9 wkts

B	2
Lbs	3
Extras	5

BOWLING ANALYSIS
Weatherspoon	11–3–51–3

Smith	12–2–54–2
Wright	8–2–40–1
Oyami	7–1–30–0

Match drawn.

AFTERMATH

Trevor Ganes and Bill Norris of Sky TV were of course on hand to interview the two captains of this remarkable game.

Ron Bridger could only remark that their batting had let the team down in their second innings, but he also had to give credit to a fine bowling performance by New Zealand.

The wicket had been good and allowed a fair contest between bat and ball, and now there remained the decider at The Oval next week.

A good crowd had remained to see the finish and while they were disappointed that England had not got over the line – they were grateful for the tailenders for holding out for a rarely drawn result.

THIRD TEST MATCH

THE OVAL
25TH JULY

The deciding match of the series had engendered a great deal of interest in the press and public. There was almost a full house half an hour before the start on a warm, muggy, and drizzly morning.

Ron Bridget and Glenn Roach came out for the toss with the president of Surrey CCC.

Both captains had decided that they would like to bat on what promised to be a very good surface. On this occasion, Ron Bridger called heads and won. He had no hesitation in signalling to the pavilion and received a very cheerful response.

A few minutes later, the New Zealand team emerged and spread out across the wet turf awaiting the two batsmen, who arrived shortly afterward, swinging their bats and looking like they meant business.

Forrest Smith and Tim Weatherspoon had managed to remain fit throughout the two series and were thirsting for a last go at the English batsman.

Ron Bridger was in an aggressive mood and twice put away slightly short balls from Forrest Smith before he slipped one precariously near to the outside edge of the bat.

Jordan Clease was, as usual, rather more circumspect but rarely missed the chance to glance or cut when the chance arose.

Thirty came up within a few overs, with both batsmen having given near chances in the slips. Tim Weatherspoon was getting some drift in from the off and finally snared Jason Clease on the front pad. It looked out and was confirmed on review.

(Clease lbw Weatherspoon 20–44 for 1)

Geoff Pearce took guard a little outside the popping crease and gave notice that he was intending to put away any overpitched intended snorkers.

Glenn Roach soon turned to his spinners and unusually gave Leslie Oyami a go with his high gloomers. Geoff Pearce relished the challenge and twice swung the ball away to leg – once for a six, which thrilled the crowd. Then he launched at a full ball, got a leading edge, and was caught in bowled expertly by the bowler diving at full stretch.

(Pearce c and c Oyami 30–80 for 2)

Such a promising start was somewhat spoiled by Ron Bridger, who, in trying to drive Forrest Smith through mid-wicket, got an unexpected lifter which looped back onto the wicket – a very unfortunate dismissal.

(Bridger b Smith 51–102 for 3)

At least in reaching fifty, Ron Bridger had brought up England's hundred.

Two new batsmen at the crease had to buckle down and play themselves in carefully.

Robert Grove was the more confident of the two,

putting away a couple of crunching drives past Leslie Oyami in the covers,

Peter Hayes preferred to watch for possible ones and twos and occasionally a twizzle – dropping the ball at his feet and taking a quick single.

Forrest Smith came back on and slipped one past Robert Grove, who replied by slapping him over square leg for four. He was not so lucky in attempting a cut, which looped to Leslie Oyami in the overs.

(Grove c Oyami b Smith 39–150 for 4)

Dudley Hardacre came in one later than his usual position. All went well for a while as he settled in, occasionally glancing to leg.

Peter Hayes then seemed to be unsighted at a fast snorker from Forrest Smith, which plucked out his off stump.

(Hayes b Smith 10–161 for 5)

Hopes of a large score were beginning to fade as Perry Hinchley came to the crease.

Dudley Hardacre had decided to proceed with caution, as both fast bowlers were getting pace and lift. The weather had now settled in steady rain, but without any damaging wind.

Dudley Hardacre played well for a time until he chanced an unwise quick run and found Leslie Oyami flicking the ball to the wicketkeeper with his bat well short of the crease.

(Hardacre run out 18–174 for 6)

Lawrence Power came in to join Perry Hinchley, and they prospered for a while as Leslie Oyami was brought back but could not find a demanding length.

Enough was enough, and Glenn Roach brought back Tim Weatherspoon, who was running in with great determination.

A fast snorker clattered into Lawrence Power's stumps.

(Power b Weatherspoon 15–191 for 7)

Roy Dukes had only just played one ball, which he pushed for a single, when Perry Hinchley went back fatally to a skidder which took him on the pads right in front.

(Hinchley lbw Weatherspoon 20–192 for 8)

The chances of England reaching 200 were not high but Robert Lincoln displayed his usual talent for the long handle, mowing two fours over long-on before he was bowled by Weatherspoon attempting a lavish drive.

(Lincoln b Weatherspoon 8–213 for 9)

Jason Smethurst eschewed his usual instinct and tried to survive to support Roy Dukes, who seemed content to push forward and nudge the odd single.

In attempting a lavish cut at a short ball from Forrest Smith, he carved into the covers. Leslie Oyami showed why he is one of the world's best fielders by diving to his right and taking the catch one-handed at full stretch.

(Smethurst c Oyami b Smith 7)

(Dukes not out 12)

Lbs 2

B3

Extras 5

England all-out 235.

NEW ZEALAND INNINGS

It was by now fairly late in the day when Glenn Roach and Joe Lymes came out to start the innings. The rain had started to fall more heavily, with gusts of wind which discomforted the batsman as well as those in the field.

Glenn Roach knew he faced a challenge with the two fast bowlers raring to go. All seemed well for a while. Glenn Roach received some wayward balls, which he put away for four to leg, and he occasionally fastened onto a waister which sat up for him to swing it to square leg.

Joe Lymes hit a couple of strong drives through mid-off and had settled in well when the two brought up the fifty. Joe Lymes then attempted a drive to Jason Smethurst which missed the bat as it swung in and took his leg stump.

(Lymes b Smethurst 27–55 for 1)

Ken Uttley joined his captain, and they played steadily for a while before Ken Uttley called for a run, was sent back by his captain and failed to beat Robert Grove's bullet throw.

(Uttley run out 12–70 for 2)

Glenn Roach was finding the conditions difficult and once or twice heaved at Perry Hinchley without making contact.

Ron Bridger brought back Robert Lincoln, seeing his discomfort, and within 3 balls speared a snorker into Glenn Roach's toes, ricocheting into his middle stump.

(Roach b Lincoln 36–78 for 3)

Joe Potter and Robert Peters came together and realised the danger of ending the day 5 wickets down.

They settled for ones and twos but Joe Potter was getting restive and eventually drove hard at Robert Lincoln and snicked to Dudley Hardacre, who took a good catch to his left at slip.

(Potter c Hardacre b Lincoln 14–93 for 4)

Leslie Ayami joined Robert Peters, and they saw out the last over of the day with enormous relief.

DAY TWO

The second day began with a light wind and spitting rain.

Robert Peters saw off the early attack of Robert Lincoln and began to play some crisp off-drives for ones and twos.

Leslie Oyami was a deal less confident. He was beaten outside off stump twice by Jason Smethurst and then steered a lucky four behind square. There was no sense of permanence there, and it was no surprise when Robert Lincoln speered one through his defence.

(Oymai b Lincoln 15–114 for 5)

Glenn Roach was looking on with rather a glum expression from the pavilion. Hopes of reaching the England score were quickly evaporating.

Peter Wright received orders from the top to defend and try to rebuild the innings. By this time, Perry Hinchley was wheeling away with a number of gloomers. He was able to deceive the batsman every now and then, but his bad balls were being put away for four rather too often for comfort.

Robert Peters then played back and was beaten through the air, and ended up with his pads right in front – no appeal necessary.

(Peters lbw Hinchley 22–130 for 6)

Vance Whearby belied his reputation by refraining

from anything excessive for a while.

Roy Dukes came on with his leg spinners but got little turn, and his length varied, enabling the batsman to milk him. Perry Hinchley was getting some turn and drift. Peter Wright had played him with apparent ease until he mistimed a drive and gave the bowler a simple caught and bowled.

(Wright c and b Hinchley 16–149 for 7)

Rory Dunes joined Vance Whearby and they held a brief conference in mid-pitch. They had evidently decided that attack was the best form of defence, and Rory Dunes left no time in hoisting both spinners for four over square leg.

By now, the rain had intensified, making battle batting more difficult.

Rory Dunes tried to drive the returning Jason Smethurst out of the ground only to get a thick edge to Dudley Hardacre in the slips.

(Dunes c Hardacre b Smethurst 10–168 for 8)

The end was not long delayed.

Forrest Smith smeared a quick two before leaving his pads in front to a fast snorker from Robert Lincoln.

(Smith lbw Lincoln 2–174 for 9)

Tim Weatherspoon held on for a short while as Vance Whearby tried to attack but he could not resist attempting a lavish drive which ended up as a caught and bowled to end the innings.

(Weatherspoon c and b Lincoln 3)

(Whearby not out 20)

Lbs 2

B 3

Extras 5

New Zealand all-out 182.

ENGLAND SECOND INNINGS

Ron Bridger and Jordan Clease came to the wicket shortly after lunch, secure in the knowledge that they had established a fifty-one run lead on the first innings.

Ron Bridger was his usual positive self and put away two well-driven fours through the covers off the first over

Jordan Clease managed a neat clip off his legs for three but then unaccountably failed to back up a sharp single and was run out by a metre, Leslie Oyami again throwing sharply to the keeper.

(Cleases run out 3–12 for 1)

This was not the start required, and Geoff Pearce played quietly in support of his captain.

The fast bowlers had, for once, not made inroads, and the score mounted steadily.

Ron Bridger brought up England's fifty with a rasping off-drive for four.

Forrest Smith was on his last over when Geoff Pearce tried a lavish cut and found Leslie Oyami waiting to pouch it at cover – a brilliant catch which left the departing batsman bemused.

(Pearce c Oyami b Smith 30–54 for 2)

Robert Grove realised that England had now gained a lead of over 100 and felt free to play a few shots at the slow bowlers.

Seeing this, Glenn Roach introduced Leslie Oyami, who served up a couple of loose ones before slipping through Robert Grove's forward defence with a lavish turner.

(Grove lbw Oyami 15–76 for 3)

Dudley Hardacre left himself no time to play himself in properly and was soon driving too early at Forrest Smith, to give him a simple caught and bowled.

(Hardacre c and b Smith 4–86 for 4)

Ron Bridger had, meanwhile, gone on his merry way and was looking quite secure when Tim Weatherspoon fired in a fast snorker which deviated just enough to beat the bat.

It had been a fine innings, and he was justly applauded by the crowd.

(Bridger b Weatherspoon 39–94 for 5)

England now had a lead approaching 150, and even without their captain, they were sure of setting a healthy target for New Zealand's second innings.

Peter Hayes and Perry Hinchley survived the last two overs of the day and retired reasonably happy.

DAY THREE

The weather had continued fairly mild overnight, with the threat of increasing wind later on.

Peter Hayes and Perry Hinchley had been told to defend sensibly but not to miss any scoring chances.

Tim Weatherspoon was a threat early on, and they played and missed several times.

Forrest Smith was mixing it up with some fast, shorter waisters dug in to shower the batsman into a false stroke. The school steadily mounted with an occasional hook for four when Tim Wetherspoon came back on with fire in his belly. He first swung a fast snorker into Peter Hayes, sending his off-stump cartwheeling.

(Hayes b Weatherspoon 22–140 for 6)

Then he turned his attention to Perry Hinchley, and Lawrence Power could only watch in admiration as he beat the batsman twice outside off stump and then brought a fast one back into his pads.

(Hinchley lbw Weatherspoon 31–147 for 7)

Roy Dukes joined Lawrence Power, and they realised that the lead was now around 200. They needed to attack if there was to be enough time left in the game to bowl New Zealand out a second time.

Roy Dukes hit a lucky couple of lofted drives for four, but Lawrence Power unwisely chanced a quick run and was beaten by Leslie Oyami's accurate throw.

(Power run out 10–167 for 8)

Robert Lincoln came and went in two balls beaten for pace by Robert Smith.

(Lincoln b Smith 0–167 for 9)

This left Rory Dukes to try the long handle, which succeeded for a while.

Jason Smethurst was aiming a lofted drive but got on top of it and returned a catch to Robert Smith to end the innings.

(Smethurst c and b Smith 1)

Dukes not out)

Lbs 2

B 3

Extras 5

England all-out 181.

NEW ZEALAND SECOND INNINGS

It was a great relief to Glenn Roach to know the winning score for which they had to aim. 236 was a long way away, particularly with the weather threatening to deteriorate later in the afternoon. He took guard with Joe Lynes limbering up at the other end.

Jason Smethurst came in with intent, gradually increasing his pace throughout the first over.

Glenn Roach left 3 balls alone and watched them pass harmlessly outside his off stump. The fourth was a wide snorker, which he steered imperiously to the cover boundary. There were no further alarms and Joe Lyons saw off Forrest Smith with a resolute defence. They progressed in ones and twos for a while, interspersed with some rasping cuts for four by the captain. By the time the slow bowlers were in tandem, they had passed fifty.

Ron Bridger decided to give Jason Smethurst a further burst, and he brought a fast skidder back into Joe Lynes' pads to have him right in front of the middle stump.

(Lynes lbw Smethurst 20–65 for 1)

Ken Uttley came in to face a fast barrage and left alone what he could.

Glenn Roach was going on his merry way, and Ken Uttley was content to pick off the occasional half-volley. He was becoming more confident when he drove uppishly and snicked to Dudley Hardacre at slip.

(Uttley c Hardacre b Lincoln 26–85 for 2)

Joe Potter was in a frisky mood, testing the field once or twice with quick singles before he overdid it and was run out from the backward point.

(Potter run out 10–99 for 3)

Leslie Oyami was not known for his stickability, but seeing that Glenn Roach was nearing his fifty, he buckled down.

Glenn Roach passed his fifty with a graceful turn off his legs to the boundary, and raised his bat to the flurry of applause from all around the ground.

Eventually, Leslie Oyami began to play his strokes and was looking promising when he drove hard and snicked to Dudley Hardacre, who leapt to his right and took the catch at arms' length.

(Oyami c Hardacre b Smethurst 18–134 for 4)

With the winning score still a hundred runs away, it was becoming crystal clear that everything now depended on Glenn Roach. Robert Peters came in to support his captain, who had now passed 70 and was still going strong.

Ron Bridger decided to gamble on his slow bowlers, and Perry Hinchley wheeled away, getting some purchase from the wicket.

Robert Peters appeared to be playing him with some ease, picking off ones and two to leg, and it was clearly time for the fast bowlers to return.

Robert Peters perished immediately to a faster ball, which took out his off stump.

(Peters b Lincoln 14–158 for 5)

Peter Wright came in realising that as the last recognised batsman, he had to play carefully as Glenn Roach continued to accumulate at the other end. He succeeded for a while and played a couple of pleasing strokes through mid-wicket for four, but then went back to a fast skidder and was bowled off his legs.

(Wright b Smith 8–180 for 6)

Vance Whearby came in, content to support his captain, who was now in the eighties.

Ron Bridger was starting to worry as the target came down to fifty runs.

Vance Whearby decided to be positive and drove Perry Hinchley for a four and a six over square leg to bring up the 200.

By now, Glenn Roach was in the nervous nineties.

Vance Whearby continued to reign in his attacking instincts until he saw a wide half-volley from Perry

Hinchley and got a thick outside edge.

Dudley Hardacre had to dive forward at full stretch to take the catch.

(Whearby c Hardacre b Hinchley 22–218 for 7)

With 18 runs to win, it was now up to Rory Dunes to hold the fort.

The score crept up, and he played and missed several times against Jason Smethurst but survived to swing a couple of short balls to the boundary.

At last, Glenn Roach reached a well-deserved century – the first by any player in the series, and raised his back to tremendous applause all around the ground.

Rory Dunes had the simple task of striking the winning runs before the two batsmen ran off into the now-pouring rain, arms around one another.

(Dunes not out 12)

(Roach not out 101)

Lb2

B3

Extras 5

New Zealand 236 for 7 wickets.

New Zealand won the test by 3 wickets.

Series results:

First test: England won

Second Test: Match drawn

Third Test: New Zealand won

TEST SERIES 1–1

ENGLAND FIRST INNINGS

R. Bridger	b Smith	51
J. Clease	lbw Weatherspoon	20
G. Pearce	c and b Oyami	30
R. Grove	c Oyami b Smith	39
D. Hardacre	run out	18
P. Hayes	b Smith	10
P. Hinchley	lbw Weatherspoon	20
L. Power	b Weatherspoon	15
R. Dukes	not out	12
R. Lincoln	b Weatherspoon	8
J. Smethurst	c Oyami b Smith	7

Total: 235 all-out

B	3
Lbs	2
Extras	5

BOWLING ANALYSIS

Smith	15–3–67–4
Weatherspoon	17–2–59–4
Oyami	12–3–54–1
Wright	11–2–50–0

NEW ZEALAND FIRST INNINGS

G. Roach	b Lincoln	36
J. Lymes	b Smethurst	27
K. Uttley	run out	12

J. Potter	c Hardacre b Lincoln	14
R. Peters	lbw Hinchley	22
L. Oyami	b Lincoln	15
P. Wright	c and b Hinchley	16
V. Whearby	not out	20
R. Dunes	c and b Smith	10
F. Smith	lbw Lincoln	2
T. Weatherspoon	c and b Lincoln	3

Total: 182 all out

B	3
Lbs	2
Extras	5

BOWLING ANALYSIS

Lincoln	14–3–48–5
Smethurst	16–2–57–2
Hinchley	14–1–35–1
Dukes	12–3–37–0

ENGLAND SECOND INNINGS

R. Bridger	b Weatherspoon	39
J. Clease	run out	3
G. Pearce	c Oyami b Smith	30
R. Grove	lbw Oyami	15
D. Hardacre	c and b Smith	4
P. Hayes	b Weatherspoon	22
P. Hinchley	lbw Weatherspoon	31
L. Power	run out	10
R. Dukes	not out	21

| R. Lincoln | b Smith | 0 |
| J. Smethurst | c and b Smith | 1 |

Total: 181 all-out

B	3
Lbs	2
Extras	5

BOWLING ANALYSIS

Weatherspoon	15–3–50–3
Smith	14–2–41–4
Oyami	12–1–45–1
Wright	10–2–40–0

NEW ZEALAND SECOND INNINGS

G. Roach	not out	101
J. Lymes	lbw Smethurst	20
K. Uttley	c Hardacre b Lincoln	26
J. Potter	run out	10
R. Peters	b Lincoln	14
L. Oyami	c and b Smith	18
P. Wright	lbw Smith	8
V. Whearby	c and b Hinchley	22
R. Dunes	not out	12

Total: 236 for 7 wkts

B	3
Lbs	2
Extras	5

BOWLING ANALYSIS

Smethurst	15–3–59–3
Lincoln	16–2–61–2
Hinchley	14–3–62–1
Dukes	12–2–49–0

AFTERMATH

Trevor Ganes and Bill Norris were on hand as usual to congratulate the winning captain and, in this case, heap praise upon Glenn Roach for his outstanding not-out innings, which had undoubtedly won the match for New Zealand.

Ron Bridger was magnanimous in admitting that his team had been thoroughly beaten this time, but he felt the series, drawn 1–1, was a very fair result and recognition of the two teams' abilities.

A cup with both teams included was held in the pavilion by the two captains.

Glenn Roach addressed a sizeable crowd who had remained, "It has been a great pleasure and privilege to play here in England again, and even more so as the games have been played in a sporting spirit and have been so close.

I think it is fair to say that rain cricket is generally a bowlers' game, but there have been some sterling batting performances on both sides, and the hospitality has been second to none.

I wish to thank the groundsmen and all the supporting staff for their sterling efforts.

I look forward to returning before too long to these shores."

Ron Bridger shook his hand before declaring:

"To play the New Zealand team has been a positive pleasure. They are a sporting and generous team and have given us a tremendous challenge.

The results have been very close, and the support of the crowd has been tremendous. We wish you and your team well on your return journey and hope and expect to see you back here before too long."

With that, the teams retired to enjoy a belated tea and a very convivial evening together.